DUST DEVIL . . . OR DOOM?

"How long has that been there?" Clint asked, pointing behind them.

Yates turned to look at Clint and reined in the team. "What?" he asked.

"That cloud of dust."

"I'm sorry, Clint," he said, hanging his head.

"Well, do you think it's them?"

"It's them," Sawyer called out. "Take my word for it, Adams. My boys will be on you by noon tomorrow."

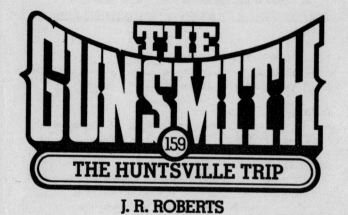

THE GUNSMITH

159

THE HUNTSVILLE TRIP

J. R. ROBERTS

J
JOVE BOOKS, NEW YORK

THE HUNTSVILLE TRIP

A Jove Book / published by arrangement with
the author

PRINTING HISTORY
Jove edition / March 1995

ISBN: 0-515-11571-1

A JOVE BOOK®
Jove Books are published by The Berkley Publishing Group,
200 Madison Avenue, New York, New York 10016.
JOVE and the "J" design are trademarks
belonging to Jove Publications, Inc.

PRINTED IN THE UNITED STATES OF AMERICA

10 9 8 7 6 5 4 3 2 1

THE GUNSMITH

159

THE HUNTSVILLE TRIP

ONE

When Clint spotted the wagon he reined Duke in and settled down to watch for a few moments.

He was a good distance from it, but he could see very clearly that it was a prison wagon. This being Texas, it was probably supposed to be on its way to Huntsville Prison. Instead, it was sitting out in the middle of nowhere.

Looking down at the wagon from atop a small rise, he could see that there were prisoners inside, although he had no way of knowing how many.

Oddly there didn't seem to be anyone else around. Where was the driver and his guard? Clint wondered. This kind of wagon load was usually accompanied by at least two men.

"Let's take a ride around, big fella," Clint said to Duke, giving the big gelding a little nudge in the ribs to get him moving.

He rode in a circle, never getting much closer to the wagon, just in case it was a trap for some passing rider—like himself. When he got into position where he could see the front of the wagon, he thought he saw something on the ground.

It looked like a body.

His first instinct was to ride down and see if he could help, but he was still wary of some kind of trap. He moved closer, but slowly, until he was able to clearly make out the shape and form of the body. It was a man, and he didn't appear to be moving. Clint stopped and watched for a few moments and finally saw some movement.

The man was alive, but for how long?

Clint decided it was time to simply ride down and see what the situation was. He did so, but remained on his guard.

"Rider comin'," Reggie Prince said. He was an enormous black man in his late twenties, who could easily snap a man's back with a bear hug—and in fact had. That was why he was in the wagon on his way to Huntsville Prison.

"About fuckin' time," Mark Lacy said. "What the hell was he waitin' for?" Lacy was a tall, reedy man in his forties whose specialty was the knife. He was so good with it that there were three reasons he was in the wagon, and they were all dead—and one of them had been a woman.

"He thinks it's a trap," the third man in the wagon said. His name was Jeff Sawyer. He was a beefy man in his thirties with large hands and a very large head that looked too big for his five-foot-eight frame. "He's just being careful."

The other two didn't know why Sawyer was in the wagon. Sawyer hadn't said, and neither had the two lawmen transporting them. What the other two prisoners did know, however, was that Sawyer was not nervous about his situation, because he believed he was never going to reach Huntsville. He believed that his men would have him sprung long before that.

"He don't know that we're locked in here?" Prince asked.

"He doesn't know anything until he gets down here," Sawyer said.

"Maybe he'll let us out," Lacy said anxiously.

Lacy and Prince were on their knees, looking out the side of the prison wagon. Sawyer, supposedly uninterested, was still seated on one of the wooden benches attached to the wide walls.

"I guess we'll just have to wait and see, won't we?" he said.

If this stranger let them out, that would be fine with him, but he still wasn't worried. His men had tried once to get him out, and they'd failed—although they'd killed the guard and shot up the lawman driving the rig—but that didn't mean they were through trying.

No, sir, not by a long shot.

TWO

When Clint reached the wagon he didn't even have time to dismount before the men in the wagon began calling to him to let them out.

"Hey, mister, get the key, huh?" one man yelled.

"Yeah, come on," another chimed in. "Let us out of here, huh?"

"Mister?" the first man said.

Clint dismounted and, ignoring their pleas, went to the fallen man. As he crouched over him he could see that the man was still breathing.

"Hey, forget him!" one of the men shouted.

"Let us out!" another called. "We're innocent."

"Yeah," the first man yelled, "I was framed."

Clint gingerly turned the man over and saw the blood on his torso. He'd been shot, but there was so much blood Clint could not readily locate the wound. The man's face was white and pasty from shock and blood loss, but his eyes fluttered open and widened when he saw Clint.

"Don't—" he said.

Hidden by the blood was the man's badge, which

indicated he was a deputy federal marshal.

"Don't—" he said again.

"Don't what?" Clint asked.

"Don't . . . don't let them out."

"Don't worry," Clint said, "I'm not about to let them out. Can you tell me where you're hit?"

"Hit—" the man gasped, "hit . . . high up . . . chest . . ."

Clint peered closely at the man and finally saw the ragged hole, which had been hidden by the bloody shirt. He'd been shot high up on the left side, away from his heart. If he'd been treated immediately the wound would not have been half as bad, but apparently he'd fallen off the wagon and simply lay there, bleeding. Lying on his face, with the wound pressed to the ground, had actually slowed the bleeding a bit.

"You got any medical supplies under your seat?" Clint asked.

"No . . . supplies," the man gasped. "Extra . . . shirt . . ."

"That'll do," Clint said. "I need something to pack that wound with so the bleeding will stop until I can get you to a doctor."

Gently, he laid the man down and then stood up and reached under the seat of the wagon.

"Hey, mister," one of the men said, his tone lower now, "you gonna let us out?"

"Not on a bet," Clint said.

"Why not?" the man demanded, his tone rising. "Hey, we're innocent!"

"Mister," Clint replied, "nobody's innocent."

He found a canvas bag under the seat and got the extra shirt out to staunch the bleeding.

He knelt by the man and tore the shirt into strips, saving a larger piece to use as a bandage. Next, he got his canteen from his saddle and tried to clean the wound as best he could, tearing away the blood-soaked shirt. Over the next few minutes he caused the man some pain, and at one point the man blacked out, but eventually Clint got a makeshift bandage tied fairly securely around the wound.

When the man came to, Clint gave him some water and laid him back down.

"How are you feeling?"

"Like shit," the man said.

"What's your name?"

"Tom Fenimore."

"I'm Clint Adams, Tom."

Recognition dawned in the man's eyes.

"I know you."

"Yeah," Clint said, "a lot of people do. Think you can tell me what happened?"

"I got three hard cases to transport to Huntsville," Fenimore said. "Along the way we got hit. My guard was killed. I managed to get away, but I was hit, too. I got this far before I guess I fell off my wagon."

"Anybody I know in the back?" Clint asked.

"I don't know," Fenimore said. "How much newspaper reading do you do?"

"Try me."

"Got a woman-killer named Mark Lacy."

"Don't know him."

"Big black man who broke another man's back in a fight. His name's Reggie Prince."

"Nope."

"Jeff Sawyer."

That got Clint's attention.

"I thought you'd know that one."

"Sawyer. What'd he get in Huntsville?"

"For murder? He's gonna hang there. It was his boys who tried to stop us. He says they're gonna get him out before we can get him to Huntsville."

"It looks like they might."

"Over my dead body," Fenimore said, and tried to sit up.

"Hey, easy," Clint said. "You're not ready for that."

"His boys could be along any minute now," Fenimore said. "We got to get moving."

"Where are you going to go?" Clint asked. "You need a doctor."

"Nearest town . . ." Fenimore said, out of breath from the exertion of trying to sit up.

"The nearest town is Culpepper," Clint said. "I was going to pass through there myself."

"Take me there," Fenimore said, grabbing Clint's arm with surprising strength.

"I intend to take you there, Marshal, don't worry," Clint said. "But not now. It'll be dark soon, and in the morning you'll be stronger— probably not strong enough to travel, but we'll have to get moving at that point, regardless."

"Got to keep moving . . ." Fenimore said, and then fainted.

"Tomorrow," Clint told the unconscious man. He stood and walked over to Duke.

"Looks like we'll be camping here tonight, big boy," he said, patting the gelding's massive neck.

"Hey, Adams?"

This was a new voice from the back of the wagon.

"Come on over here a minute."

Clint walked over so he could see in the wagon. One man was pressed up against the back door, his face framed by the barred window. The other two were behind him.

"You know me?" Clint asked.

"I heard you introduce yourself to the lawman," the man said. "You know who I am?"

"Sawyer."

"That's right," the prisoner said. "You know what's good for you, Gunsmith, you'll let me out of here."

"Guess I don't know what's good for me, then, Sawyer," Clint said, " 'cause you and your friends are staying right where you are."

"These ain't my friends, Adams," Sawyer said. "My friends are out there, looking for me, and when they find me they'll let me out of here. If you're still around, you won't be around for long . . . if you get my meaning."

"I get it," Clint said. "You and your girlfriends better settle down and get some sleep, Sawyer. We're going to get an early start in the morning."

"Hey," one of the other men yelled. It was the other white man, Lacy. "Are you gonna feed us?"

"I might have some dried beef jerky for you," Clint said, "if you quiet down and stop chewing my ear off about letting you out."

"Oh, don't worry about that, Adams," Sawyer said. "I can see that you have no intentions of doing that. We won't be bothering you anymore."

"Good," Clint said.

"How about some coffee with that jerky?" Sawyer asked.

"Don't push your luck," Clint said, and walked away to find the makings of a camp fire.

THREE

Instead of trying to move the prone lawman, Clint instead moved the wagon away from him. He unhitched the two-horse team and picketed them away from the camp, along with Duke. He got a blanket and covered Tom Fenimore, who drifted in and out of consciousness.

When the camp was set up, he got a few pieces of beef jerky and walked over to the wagon.

"Here you go," he said, and tossed them through the bars.

"Feeding the animals, huh, Adams?" Sawyer asked, picking a piece of jerky off the floor and biting into it.

"Be grateful you're getting something," Clint replied.

"How about that coffee?"

"No way," Clint said. "I'm not getting that close to you fellas."

"You ain't afraid, are you, Adams?" Sawyer asked with a sneer in his tone.

"Just careful," Clint said, refusing to take the bait. "I'll toss you a canteen and you can pass it around and drink from it."

"I ain't drinkin' from the same canteen as some nigger," Mark Lacy complained.

"The marshal told me what Prince was in for, Lacy," Clint said. "Knowing that, I don't think I'd be talking that way if I was you."

Clint walked and left Lacy looking warily at Reggie Prince, who was chewing on a piece of jerky and grinning broadly.

Clint made a habit of carrying two canteens. He got one of them now—the less full one—walked back to the wagon and tossed it through the side bars. There was more room there than in the small window on the back door.

After that he went back to the camp fire and had himself some beans and coffee. He kept his eye on the marshal the whole time, and the man finally came awake and seemed ready to stay that way for a while.

"Want to try and eat something?" he asked.

It took Fenimore's eyes a moment to focus and his brain a moment to register what was happening before he could answer.

"I think so," he said then.

Clint spooned some beans into a dish and moved over by the lawman.

"How about sitting up?" he asked.

"I'll give it a try."

"Let me help you."

With Clint's help Fenimore got into a seated position, and Clint proceeded to feed him some beans.

"Sorry, but beans is all I have left," he said.

"Don't apologize," Fenimore said. "It's fine."

"What's a deputy marshal doing transporting prisoners?" Clint asked as he fed the man. "I thought they had men for that dirty job."

"Sawyer," Fenimore said. "They really want to get him to Huntsville, and they thought a deputy might have a better chance of getting him there. Guess they were wrong."

"Hey," Clint said, "there's still time."

"I really botched this job up."

"If you weren't there," Clint said, "maybe there'd be another dead man and three escaped prisoners. Did you ever think of that?"

"Well, no," Fenimore said, "I didn't . . . but then I haven't had much time to think about anything."

"Well, that's true," Clint said. "You sure haven't."

After the lawman had finished all the beans, Clint asked, "Want to try some coffee?"

"Sure," Fenimore said. "Why not, while I'm sitting up?"

Clint poured a cup and handed it to the man, who held it in both hands and sipped gratefully.

"I wish I had some whiskey to put in there."

"Take a look under the seat."

"In your bag?"

Fenimore shook his head.

"Just under the seat."

Clint walked to the wagon and felt around under the seat until his fingers touched something smooth. He hauled it out and found a half-filled bottle of whiskey. He walked back to the camp fire, tipped some into the deputy's coffee, and then some into a cup for himself.

"If I'd known this was there," he said, "I could have used it to clean your wound."

"I'm glad you didn't waste it on that," Fenimore said. "I think the inner man needs it more."

They drank in silence until Fenimore was done, and by that time the man's eyes were drooping.

"Ready to lie back down?" Clint asked.

"I think so," Fenimore said. "I feel like the roof's about to cave in."

Clint helped the man lie back down. He'd decided to give the deputy his saddle for a pillow, and covered him with the blanket.

"We got to talk in the morning," Fenimore said.

"We will," Clint said. Then, as an afterthought, he added, "About what?"

"About you taking these men to Huntsville for me," the deputy said.

"What?"

There was no answer.

"Hey, Fenimore, forget it—" Clint started, but he stopped when he realized the man was unconscious.

Well, in the morning he'd tell him that there wasn't a chance in hell that he was going to replace him and take the prisoners to Huntsville.

Not a snowball's chance in hell!

FOUR

Clint slept with one eye open that night. He knew he couldn't stay awake all night keeping watch, but he tried to sleep as lightly as possible, knowing Jeff Sawyer's men were wandering around looking for them.

He was awake and breaking camp when Tom Fenimore opened his eyes.

"What?" Fenimore said. "No breakfast?"

"Culpepper's not that far from here," Clint said. "We can eat when we get there—and after you've been tended to by a real doctor. How do you feel?"

"Better," Fenimore said, "but not by much."

"Well, you'll feel a lot better when we get you to town."

"How've they been?" Fenimore asked, with a jerk of his head toward the wagon.

"They've been quiet since I told them I wasn't letting them out."

"I guess I was pretty lucky it was you that happened along," Fenimore said. "Somebody else might have let them out, and then I would have been finished."

14

"Think they would have killed you?"

"I think Sawyer would have been on his way," Fenimore said. "The other two though, they would have taken their anger out on me."

Clint gave Fenimore the last cup of coffee and then went to hitch up the team to the wagon.

"Good morning, Adams," Jeff Sawyer said. "What kind of a night did you have? Not too restful, I bet. Sleep with one eye open, did you?"

Clint did not reply to any of Sawyer's jibes, so the man fell silent. Not so the other two, though.

"Hey, Adams, come on," Lacy said. "Time to let us out, huh?"

"Why you got to help that lawman?" Reggie Prince asked. "I don't get it, fella. What you want to put us away for?"

"I'm not putting you fellas away," Clint said. "You did that yourselves."

"Hey, Adams . . . hey . . ." Lacy called, but Clint walked away from the wagon.

He saddled Duke next, then took Fenimore's empty coffee cup and stowed it away with the rest of his dwindling supplies.

The next step was to get Fenimore up on the wagon again. He claimed he was up to driving the team. It took a while, and Fenimore sucked in his breath a couple of times in pain before they finally got him in position. Once the marshal was up there, Clint climbed up and checked his wound to make sure they hadn't started it bleeding again.

"You sure you're going to be able to sit up here for a few miles?" Clint asked. "I can probably strap you in—"

"Don't worry," Fenimore said. "I'll make it."

"If you feel at any time that you're going to fall off, sing out," Clint said. "I'll be riding alongside, and I'll catch you."

"I'll make it—if Sawyer's men don't find us first."

"If that happens," Clint said, "you'll have to drive the wagon as hard as you can while I hold them off."

At the moment the reins were sitting loosely in Fenimore's hands, but at Clint's words his hands tightened on them.

"Don't worry," he said again.

"I'm not," Clint said. "Oh, listen, about what you said last night?"

"What did I say?"

"You know, just before you, uh, fell asleep?"

Fenimore frowned and said, "I don't remember saying anything. What did I say?"

Clint thought about repeating it to the man, then decided it was just as well Fenimore had forgotten.

"Never mind," he said, "it wasn't important."

FIVE

Culpepper was not much of a town, and the thing that annoyed Clint the most was the lack of telegraph wires. He had hoped to be able to wire for help for Fenimore from Huntsville. Traveling on horseback, the trip from Culpepper to Huntsville would probably take two days at the most. However, traveling by prison wagon, the trip could take as long as four days. Clint didn't think Fenimore was anywhere near being in shape to make the trek. Once again he was glad the lawman had forgotten what he'd said the night before—but how long would it be before the idea occurred to him a second time?

Fenimore was wobbly when they arrived, and Clint felt that even another half a mile would have been too much for the man.

"Excuse me," Clint said to a man who was crossing the street.

The man had been trying to get a look inside the prison wagon, as had most of the townspeople they'd passed.

"Where's the doctor?"

"Doc Gates," the man said, pointing. "Another block, on the right. Can't miss it."

"Thanks."

"Mister," the man asked, "you got any killers inside?"

"All the time," Clint said.

When they got to the doctor's office, Clint dismounted just in time to catch Fenimore as he toppled off the wagon seat.

"Hey, Adams," Jeff Sawyer called out, "you just going to leave us out here?"

"You'll be safe," Clint said, and carried Fenimore into the office.

To the doctor's credit, he reacted quickly.

"Take him inside," the man said, coming around his desk.

He opened the door to a second room, and Clint carried Fenimore in. The doctor, a tall, white-haired man who looked to be in his sixties, immediately went to work.

"Gunshot," he said, talking to himself. Turning to Clint he asked, "When?"

"Sometime yesterday."

The doctor turned and held something out to Clint.

"Hold on to this," he said, handing Clint the man's badge.

Clint looked at the bloodstained hunk of metal and then stuck it in his pocket.

"You better get out of here and let me get to work," the doctor said.

"I'll be back later, Doctor."

The man didn't answer. He was engrossed in tending to Fenimore's wound.

Clint went back outside, where a crowd had gathered around the prison wagon.

Inside the wagon Sawyer was hissing at the people, like a caged animal, trying to scare them—and succeeding, in the case of some women and small children.

"Excuse me," Clint said. "Can I get through?"

"These men your responsibility?" someone asked.

Clint turned and saw a man wearing a sheriff's badge staring at him.

"Not exactly," Clint said.

"What does that mean?"

"The man driving them is inside," Clint said. "He's got a bullet in him. There was a second man, but he's dead."

"Who's inside?" the sheriff asked.

Clint took the bloodstained badge from his pocket and handed it to the sheriff.

"Deputy Marshal Tom Fenimore," Clint said. "He was taking these men to Huntsville."

The sheriff took the badge and stared down at it.

"What's your name?" the man asked.

"Clint Adams."

"I'm Sheriff Calvin Gage," the man said, sticking his hand out. Clint shook it. "You want to put these men up at my jail?"

"Sounds like a good idea."

"Come on, then," Gage said.

He turned to the crowd and shouted, "Nothing to see here, folks. Be on your way." When very few people moved, Gage shouted, "I said, get moving!"

After that the crowd started to disperse.

Clint climbed atop the wagon, grabbed the reins, and followed the sheriff, who walked ahead. Duke was left standing in front of the doctor's office. Clint knew the big gelding wasn't going anywhere.

When they reached the sheriff's office, Clint climbed down.

"Who you got in there?" the sheriff asked.

"According to the marshal, Jeff Sawyer and two others," Clint said.

That stopped the sheriff.

"Sawyer?"

"That's right."

The man looked nervous.

"Something wrong?"

"Damn right," Gage said. "Sawyer's gang is sure to want to break him out. I don't need that kind of trouble in this town."

"What town would you suggest the marshal take his trouble to, Sheriff?"

Gage didn't answer.

"You going to put these men in your jail or not?"

Gage scowled and said, "Yeah, I am. Where's the damn key?"

Clint had taken it from Fenimore the night before.

"Here," he said, and handed it to the sheriff. "Like it or not, as a sworn-in lawman, these men are your responsibility now."

SIX

When the three men were placed in cells—
Prince and Lacy in one, to Lacy's dismay, and
Sawyer in a cell of his own—Clint and the sheriff
sat down at the sheriff's desk.

"I don't like this," Gage said.

"Well, neither do I."

"These men are not my responsibility."

"Well, they're more yours than mine, I'd say,"
Clint replied.

"How bad is this deputy marshal hurt?"

"I don't know," Clint said. "You'll have to ask
your town doctor that. He's working on him right
now."

"Is he gonna be able to take these men on to
Huntsville?"

"I doubt it," Clint said. "The kind of wound he
has takes weeks to heal."

"Damn it!" Gage said. "I ain't keepin' these
men here all that time. Sawyer's gang will take
this town apart."

"You won't have to keep them that long," Clint
said. "I'm sure the prison will be sending someone

to take over for him. If you had a telegraph office it would be easy to notify them."

"We been tryin' to get one," the sheriff complained. "Money, you know?"

"Sure," Clint said. "What's the nearest town that does have a telegraph?"

The sheriff thought a minute and then said, "Probably Brockton."

"How far?"

"A day's ride."

"That far?"

"We're not exactly on the main path," Gage said. "That's our big problem, what's probably gonna keep us from growin' much bigger than we are now."

Clint wasn't in the mood to sympathize with the town's plight at the moment.

"Well," Gage said, "before we argue over whose responsibility they are I better go over to the doc's and see how the deputy marshal is doin'."

Funny, Clint thought, I thought we already argued about it.

"That's fine," he said, standing up. "I'm going to get a room at the hotel, and then a decent meal."

"You can get both at the hotel," the sheriff said, also standing up and reaching for his hat.

"Which hotel?"

Gage gave Clint a look and said, "We only got one."

"Right."

SEVEN

Clint walked Duke over to the livery, then went to the Culpepper Hotel. He was registering his name in the book when he realized that he hadn't gotten Tom Fenimore's badge back from the sheriff. He'd have to remember to ask him for it. That he did feel responsible for.

"Do you have facilities for a bath?" he asked the clerk.

"Of course we do, sir," the man said, looking insulted. "We might be a small town, but we do have all the amenities."

"All I want's a bath," Clint said. "Could you have one drawn for me? I'll be right down."

"Immediately, sir."

Clint took his gear up to his room, pulled out a fresh shirt, and took it downstairs with him. A bath was going to feel mighty good.

Freshly bathed, Clint went directly to the dining room for a hot meal. He ordered steak and potatoes, and while he'd had better, the meal sat just fine with him. He had a pot of coffee with it, and then followed it with a second pot. Feeling satiated, he left the hotel and walked over to the doctor's office. When Clint entered, the man was seated behind his desk.

"Doctor," Clint said, "we didn't get a chance to meet properly before."

"There was no time," the doctor said, standing up. "Your friend needed immediate attention."

"Clint Adams," Clint said, extending his hand.

"Dr. Augustus Gates," the man said. "Your quick work with that makeshift bandage might have saved your friend's life."

"He's not really my friend, Doctor," Clint said and explained to the man how he had found Deputy Marshal Tom Fenimore.

"Well, he's doubly lucky to be alive, then," Gates said, when Clint was finished. "If he'd had to lie there a little longer he would have died."

"How is he now?"

"He's in the back and he's stable," the doctor said. "I don't have room for him here though. He's going to have to be moved to the hotel."

"Do you want me to—"

"No, no," the doctor said, interrupting him, "it won't be necessary for you to do it. I'll have someone take him over."

"I suppose the state of Texas will be paying his bills," Clint said.

"Which probably means I'll never see a cent," the doctor said. "Oh well, why should they be any different from anyone else?"

"Can I talk to him?"

"Let me see if he's awake."

The doctor went into the other room and returned almost immediately.

"He's awake, but don't talk to him for very long. He's lost a lot of blood."

"Thanks, Doc."

Clint entered the room, and the doctor closed the door behind him. Fenimore was lying on a table that was against the left wall, his feet closest to Clint.

"Clint," Fenimore said.

Clint walked to the table and looked down at Fenimore. He was pale, but he looked better than Clint had seen him before.

"How are you feeling?"

"Pretty good, now that I'm patched up," Fenimore said. "Where are the prisoners?"

"They're in the local jail," Clint said. "The sheriff's a little nervous about having Sawyer there, though."

"I don't blame him," Fenimore said. "Sawyer's men would take this town apart to get to him. We'll have to get him and the others out of here as soon as possible."

"There's no telegraph in town, Tom," Clint said. "The only way to get help is to ride to Brockton and use theirs. I'll go and send a wire to the prison—"

"There's no time for that," Fenimore said. "Sawyer's gang will find him here, Clint, I know it. The only way to keep them from getting to him is to stay ahead of them."

"You can't do that, Tom," Clint said. "You're going to have to spend a good amount of time in bed, recovering."

"You'll have to do it for me, then," Fenimore said.

I knew it, Clint thought.

"Now wait—"

"It's the only answer, Clint," Fenimore said. "I'll deputize you, and you can wear my badge. You've got to get Sawyer to Huntsville."

"Tom, I can't do it," Clint said. "I'll ride to Brockton and send the wire, but that's it."

"Clint," Fenimore said, grabbing hold of Clint's arm, "you have to help me."

"What's the all-fired hurry, Tom?" Clint asked. "There's no reason to believe that Sawyer's gang will track us here, and all he's got waiting for him at Huntsville is a rope."

"Look," Fenimore said, "I'm the one who caught him, Clint, I'm the one who put him away. I've got to make sure he gets what's coming to him. Do you understand?"

"Frankly," Clint said, "no. Is this a personal thing, Tom? I mean, more than the fact that it was you who caught him?"

Fenimore released Clint's arm and turned his face to the wall. He seemed to be steeling himself for something, and Clint gave him time. When he turned his head back again he seemed ready.

"He killed my wife."

Clint didn't know what to say to that.

"I have a small ranch, which is where I live

when I'm not working," Fenimore said. "Sawyer knew I was on his trail, so he went there and . . . and he and his men raped and then killed my wife."

"Do you know for sure it was them?"

"Oh, I know," Fenimore said. "The son of a bitch left a note pinned on her torn clothing."

Clint felt a shiver run up and down his spine. No wonder Fenimore wanted to get Sawyer to the gallows.

"I'm asking you, Clint," Fenimore said, "begging you. See that he gets there."

At this point, with the story Fenimore told, Clint didn't see that he had any other choice.

"Okay, Tom," he said, "I'll do it."

"Promise?"

Clint sighed.

"I promise."

EIGHT

Clint was in the saloon later on that afternoon, nursing a beer. The place was half full at this time of the day, and he was surprised to see two saloon girls circulating. One of them spotted him and walked over, her full hips swaying. Her bosom was impressive and was almost overflowing from the bodice of her dress. She had hair as black as coal, pale skin, and a dark blue dress that did wonders for the whole package. He was planning to turn her away, but as she got closer and her perfume reached him first, teasing him, he felt something stirring in his groin.

"You're new," she said.

"That's right."

"Staying in town long?"

"Not long."

Her eyes were brown, set slightly too wide apart above a straight nose. She appeared to be in her early thirties, just beginning to show the wear of her profession, but still a very handsome and sensual woman.

"You like me, don't you?" she asked.

He was taken aback by her aggressiveness.

"I don't know you."

"But you like what you see, right?"

He saw no reason to deny it.

"Oh, yes."

"My name is Daphne."

"A lovely name."

"What's yours?"

"Clint."

"Ooh," she said, "a strong name. Are you a strong man, Clint?"

"I get by."

"What about your . . . stamina?"

They were playing a game, he knew, fencing, but not the way she fenced with most of the patrons. With them he thought she would swoop in, ask if they wanted company, and then move on to the next one if the answer was no.

This was different.

She seemed just as interested in him as he was in her.

"Look," she said, "I get off work here at nine."

"I don't, uh, pay—"

"Let's stop the games," she said. "It's very rare that a man walks in here and catches my eye. Hell, it's been rare my whole life. When it does happen, though, I don't like to let opportunities go to waste. Do you know what I mean?"

He did. It was exactly the way he felt.

"I do."

"Are you at the hotel?"

"Yes."

"Would you like to see me tonight?"

"Yes, I would."

"What's your last name?"

"Adams."

"All right, then," she said, and abruptly walked away.

He assumed they had just made some kind of date.

A minute later Sheriff Calvin Gage came walking in. He came over and stood next to Clint at the bar.

"Tim, a beer," he said to the bartender. When he had his drink, the sheriff turned and looked at Clint. "I talked to your friend."

"When?"

"Just a little while ago," Gage said. "He's at the hotel, you know."

"I knew he was going to be moved there, but I didn't know it had been done already."

"Well, it has," Gage said, and sipped his beer. Clint swirled what was left of his around the bottom of his mug. "He told me you and him talked, and you're takin' the prisoners on to Huntsville."

"It looks that way."

"You don't sound happy about it."

"I'm not."

"Then why do it?"

"Because he asked me to."

"That a good enough reason?"

"Between me and him it is."

"Suit yourself," Gage said. "I don't know if I'd

want to go up against Sawyer's gang just because somebody asked me to."

"That makes you a smart man," Clint said.

"When do you think you'll be leavin'?" the sheriff asked.

"I have to talk to Fenimore again," Clint said. "Probably in the morning."

"The sooner the better," Gage said.

Clint looked at him.

"I meant, for you," the man hurriedly added.

"I know what you meant, Sheriff."

Gage looked nervous, not sure whether or not he'd insulted Clint.

"Can I buy you another beer?"

It occurred to Clint that he hadn't seen the lawman pay for the one he had.

"No," Clint said, "I've got to get going. Might as well have that talk with Fenimore now."

"You just tell me when you want them prisoners," Gage said.

"I'll be sure to let you know."

"Appreciate that."

Clint turned to leave, then turned back.

"One more thing, Sheriff."

"What's that?"

"Fenimore's badge?" Clint asked. "I gave it to you in your office."

"Oh, sure," Gage said. He reached into his shirt pocket and took out the bloodied badge. "Here ya go."

Clint accepted it, turning it over in his hand. He walked over to his beer mug, which still had about half an inch of liquid at the bottom. It was enough for his purposes. He dropped the badge into it, swished it around, then fished it out and shook it off. It was clean now, all of the blood mixed with the beer at the bottom of the mug. He dropped the badge into his shirt pocket, figuring it would dry off in there.

"Thanks."

NINE

Clint nodded and went outside. Part of him almost wished Sawyer's gang would come riding in now, or during the night, to set Sawyer free. At least then it would be settled and he wouldn't have to make the journey. But most likely he'd be leaving in the morning with the three prisoners, hoping to get to Huntsville in one piece.

"How can he sleep?" Mark Lacy asked aloud, looking at Jeff Sawyer in the other cell.

"Why not?" Reggie Prince asked. "He's gonna hang. It'll all be over for him real soon. We got time to do."

"I'm not going to hang," Sawyer said without moving. He was lying on his back with one arm across his face.

"Oh, that's right," Prince said, "your boys are gonna get you out."

"That's right."

"They did such a good job the first time," Prince went on.

Sawyer moved his arm and looked over at Prince and Lacy.

"You keep flapping your mouth," he said to the big black man, "when they do bust me out I'll tell them to leave you in."

"You'll take me out with you, won't you, Sawyer?" Lacy asked.

Sawyer studied Lacy for a few moments and then said, "Maybe," and put his arm back across his face.

"Yeah," Prince said, "he'll leave me and take you, because you're so smart."

"Okay, so I ain't so smart," Lacy said, "but I don't keep, uh, flapping my mouth like you do."

"Seems to me you flap your mouth more than anybody," Prince said, glaring at the smaller white man. "Seems to me you don't stop to think before you talk, neither."

Lacy was about to reply when he stopped and thought for a moment. Being in the same cell with Prince, it wouldn't be smart to talk back to him. After all, Prince was going to prison for breaking a man's back.

"Well, that's better," Prince said to him. "If you stop to think first, you'll say less things that will get you in trouble."

Lacy glared at Prince, but still didn't talk back to him.

"Okay, Sawyer," Prince said, moving to the set of bars between their cells, "when will your boys be comin'?"

"Soon," Sawyer said.

"How soon?" Prince asked.

"Soon enough," Sawyer said. "Don't worry about it, Prince."

"I am worried about it," the big man said. "We could've got killed when your men started shooting it out with the guard. What's gonna happen next time?"

"I don't know," Sawyer said. "I guess that's going to be up to them, isn't it?

"Can you trust these boys of yours?"

"Oh yeah," Sawyer said, "I rode with these boys a long time. I can trust them."

"Yeah," Prince muttered, sitting down on his bunk, "trust them to get us killed. What do you think, Lacy?"

"Me?"

"Yeah, you," Prince said. "I'm asking you what you think, now. Ain't you got no opinion?"

Lacy looked back at Prince, at the man's massive hands, and couldn't decide what to say.

"What's the matter now?" Prince demanded. "Cat got your tongue?"

Lacy looked around and said, "I don't see no cat."

"You sassin' me, boy?" the black man asked.

"I ain't sassin' nobody," Lacy muttered.

"Why don't you both just get some sleep," Sawyer said. "I get the feeling we'll be traveling early tomorrow morning."

"What kind of feelin'?" Prince demanded.

"Just a feeling," Sawyer said, without moving his arm. "Go to sleep, damn it."

"Hey, Sawyer—" Lacy started, but Prince cut him off.

"Didn't you hear the man?" he shouted. "Let's get some sleep."

Lacy lay down on his bunk with his back to Prince, then thought better of it and turned around so he could keep an eye on the black man.

TEN

At nine-fifteen that night there was a knock on Clint's hotel room door.

Daphne came in and, true to what she'd said about not wasting opportunities, she was all over him. She was as aggressive here as she had been in the saloon, and while he normally preferred to be the aggressive one, he decided to let this woman have her way.

And she did.

She literally stripped him naked, and even before she had removed her dress she was on her knees in front of him, licking his penis with long, eager strokes.

"You like gentle women?" she asked, looking up from between his legs.

"Sometimes."

"And long, easy sex?" She nuzzled his jutting erection with the tip of her nose, finding the extra sensitive spot just below the head and making him jump.

"Sometimes."

"Well," she said, smiling lewdly, "this ain't gonna be one of those times. . . ."

• • •

She kept her word. The first time was hard and fast and rough. He knew that she had left some scratches on his back and some bite marks on other parts of his body, but he had been so caught up in the excitement himself that he'd barely felt them at the time they were inflicted.

The second time they made love was slower, easier, and she proved just as adept at that style of sex as the first. First she had straddled him, taking him inside of her, but then he turned her over and explored her with his mouth, starting below her waist. In fact, he had started at her feet, sucking on her toes, licking the soles of her feet, and then working his way up her legs. She told him that no man had ever started that way before, and he felt her excitement mounting as he reached the smooth skin of her thighs with his mouth. He spread her legs, kissed and lightly bit the tender flesh there, then moved his tongue upward until he was licking her moist vagina with long, slow strokes of his tongue.

"Oh, Jesus . . ." she said after a few moments of that and then began to buck beneath him, her breath coming in deep gasps as she fought the urge to scream.

He mounted her right then, and she wrapped her powerful thighs around him, locking her ankles and rocking with him until they were both gasping. . . .

• • •

"You leavin' today?" she asked, watching from the bed as he dressed the next morning before dawn.

"I have to," he said, pulling on his boots.

"Well, then," she said, rolling onto her back and putting her hands behind her head, "I'm glad we decided not to play games."

The position did interesting things for her breasts, which were surprisingly firm for their size.

He walked over to the bed, leaned over and kissed first one nipple, then the other, lingering just for a second over each with his tongue, just long enough for her to moan and squeeze her thighs together.

"So am I," he said, and then kissed her mouth.

ELEVEN

Clint went to the livery to check on the prison wagon.

"Be needin' it today?" the liveryman asked.

"And soon," Clint said. He handed the man some money and asked, "Would you hitch up the team and get the wagon out front for me?"

"What about the gelding?" the man asked. "Want me to saddle it, too?"

"I'll do that myself."

"Suit yourself."

Clint left the livery and walked to the sheriff's office. He figured with prisoners in the cells the man would have spent the night, or at least split the night with a deputy. When he got there he was pleased to see Gage himself there. He looked like he, too, had just woken up.

"It's barely light," the sheriff said, "but I figured you'd be here early. Got the wagon outside?"

"Not yet," Clint said. "I just came to talk to them first."

"About what?"

"About what's expected of them during the trip. Can I go back?"

The sheriff yawned and said, "Go ahead."

Clint walked into the back and stood in front of Sawyer's cell. He saw that the man was already awake.

"Well, well, look who's here," Sawyer said. "Morning, Adams. Come to say good-bye?"

"I came to tell the three of you that I'll be taking you on to Huntsville," Clint said.

"You?" Sawyer asked. "You ain't no lawman."

"That's right, I'm not," Clint said, "so listen up. I'm doing this as a favor to the deputy, but I won't be wearing a badge, which means that I'm not bound to treat you as well as he might have."

"He didn't treat us well," Mark Lacy groused.

"Well," Clint said, "I'll treat you at least as well as he did, providing we understand one another."

"What's to understand?" Reggie Prince asked. The conversation had brought him awake last.

"I'll kill the first man who steps out of line."

None of the three men said a word.

"Did you hear me?"

"We heard," Sawyer said.

"What's that mean?" Reggie Prince asked. "Step out of line?"

"The first man who looks like he's not going to cooperate or is going to give me trouble."

"And you'll just kill whoever it is?" Prince asked.

"One bullet," Clint said, touching his forefinger to the center of his forehead, "right here. It'll be over quick and easy."

Sawyer laughed, and both Prince and Lacy looked over at him.

"What's so funny?" Prince asked him.

"He's bluffing."

"How can you tell?" Lacy asked.

"He can't just kill us and get away with it," Sawyer said.

"I can if I say the dead man was trying to escape," Clint said.

"It would be your word against the other two," Sawyer said.

Clint grinned what he hoped was an unfriendly grin.

"Who would they believe, Sawyer?" he asked. "Me or you?"

Prince and Lacy seemed to be waiting for Sawyer to answer the question.

"Now, you," Clint said to Sawyer, "you've got some rules all your own."

"Like what?"

"Like if I see the slightest sign of your boys, I'm going to kill you and leave your body for them. That way, everybody gets what they want."

Sawyer snorted.

"You kill me and they'll hunt you down."

"I don't think so," Clint said. "With you dead, I think they'd just forget all about the prison wagon. They wouldn't have any reasons left to risk their own lives."

"To avenge me."

"You're forgetting the kind of men you run around with, Sawyer," Clint said. "Are you expecting some thirst for honor out of them? Or vengeance? I don't think so. Getting you out alive would do them some good, because you're a good planner. Once you're dead, though, I think they'd just go on with their own lives."

Clint started to walk out, then turned back to Sawyer and asked, "What do you think?"

He walked back into the office, where the sheriff was sitting at his desk, smiling.

"You think they bought all of that?" he asked.

"I think they've got something to think about now," Clint said.

"You plan on takin' them all the way to Huntsville by yourself?" Gage asked.

Clint turned to face him.

"Unless you're offering to go along."

"Oh no," Gage said, "I got enough work here to keep me busy. 'Sides, I don't have a death wish."

"Then I guess I'm taking them by myself."

Gage rubbed his jaw and said, "There is somebody in town who might go along—if you ask him right, that is."

"Who is it?" Clint asked. "And what's the right way to ask him? Money?"

"No," Gage said, "not money. You'd have to get him interested, is all. See, he gets bored easy. If you get him interested he just might volunteer to go along."

"Well, who is this bored person and how do I get him interested?"

"Meet me at the saloon in an hour and I'll see if I can't arrange an introduction."

"It's a little early for the saloon to be open, isn't it?" Clint asked.

"Trust me," Gage said, "it'll be open."

TWELVE

"He was serious," Lacy said.

"He's just trying to scare us," Sawyer said.

"He done a good job," Lacy said.

"I ain't scared of him," Prince said. "I ain't scared of no man."

"That's where you're wrong," Sawyer said. "This man you should be afraid of."

"Why?" Lacy asked. "You just said yourself he was bluffing."

"About killing us in cold blood, yes, he is," Sawyer said, "but not about getting us to Huntsville. He really means that."

"I ain't goin' to no white man's jail," Prince said. "If I gets my chance I'm damn well takin' it, no matter what he says."

"We don't have to worry about that, Prince," Lacy said. Then he looked at Sawyer and asked, "Your boys will see to that, won't they, Sawyer?"

"Yeah," Sawyer said, sounding less confident than he had previously, "they'll see to it."

Then he added to himself. They better.

Getting him away from some deputy marshal who was more sand than brains was one thing, but breaking him free of Clint Adams, the Gunsmith—that was going to be another thing.

Yeah, he thought again, they damn well had better do the job right next time.

THIRTEEN

Clint was interested in what the sheriff had to say only because it made sense to have some help in transporting the prisoners. After all, even the wounded Deputy Marshal Fenimore had taken help along.

Clint stopped by the general store to pick up some supplies, wondering idly who was going to cover his expenses for this trip. He was also wondering whether he should take Duke along or leave him behind. Leaving him behind would mean, of course, returning to this town to retrieve him.

After stocking up on supplies he went back to the hotel to check on the deputy marshal. He thought about getting a key from the desk and letting himself in, but if Fenimore was awake that might get him shot. It was a better idea to knock on the door, even if it meant waking the man up.

"Come in," Fenimore's voice called in response to the knock.

"Good morning, Tom," Clint said, closing the door behind him.

"Mornin', Clint," Fenimore said. Clint noticed that the man had his gun in his hand, resting on top of the bed covers. As Clint approached, Fenimore placed the gun beneath the covers and brought his hand out empty.

"How are you feeling?" Clint asked.

"I'm not sure," Fenimore said, frowning. "I woke up only a few minutes before you knocked."

"Tom," Clint said, "I'll be leaving today. I've already gotten some supplies."

"I'll make sure your expenses are covered, Clint," Fenimore promised.

Clint simply nodded in reply to that, even though he'd been thinking about it himself just moments before.

"Are you going alone?" Fenimore asked.

"I'm not sure," Clint said. "I was planning to, but the sheriff asked me the same question. Seems he has someone in mind to ride along."

"I don't know if I can get anyone to cover that expense, Clint," Fenimore said. "If not . . . hell, I'll pay it myself."

"That might not be necessary, Tom," Clint said. "The sheriff seems to feel that this fellow he has in mind might volunteer."

"Too bad," Fenimore said, "I was hoping it would be somebody smart."

Clint smiled at that.

"Anyway, I don't think I'll be back up to see you before I leave."

"Good luck, then," Fenimore said, extending

his hand, "and thanks, Clint. I can't tell you how much this means to me."

Clint shook the man's hand.

"Thank me when I get Sawyer to Huntsville," he said. "When I reach a town with a telegraph I'll send a wire ahead and tell them what happened."

"I don't know if that's such a good idea, Clint."

"Why not?"

"A prison wagon in any town starts tongues waggin'," Fenimore said. "You'll leave a clear trail that way."

"What do you suggest?"

"Don't stop unless you really need supplies bad," the deputy marshal said. "That's just my advice."

"Informed advice, at that," Clint said. "I'll keep it in mind."

He started for the door then turned when Fenimore called out, "Clint?"

"Yes?"

"My plan, if Sawyer's men caught up to us, was to kill him before I let them set him free."

Clint stared at the injured lawman.

"That was my plan," Fenimore said again.

Clint nodded and said, "I'll keep that in mind, Tom."

FOURTEEN

Fenimore's words rang in Clint's ears as he left the hotel. The lawman was telling him to kill Sawyer before allowing his men to break him free. Clint didn't know if he'd be able to do that, not even knowing what crimes the man had committed. Shooting a man in cold blood was something very personal, he believed, something a man could only do to another man who had caused him great harm or grief.

In the case of Tom Fenimore it was both. First the deputy's wife had been raped and killed, and now the man himself was injured.

Clint, on the other hand, was simply doing a favor for the deputy, a favor that was motivated by . . . what? Certainly not friendship, for they had only met yesterday. By what, then? A sense of justice?

Whatever the reason, he had committed himself to seeing that Sawyer and the other two got to Huntsville Prison to serve their sentences. Beyond that, he had no obligation.

Tom Fenimore could do his own killing.

• • •

Clint walked to the saloon and, as the sheriff had promised, it was open. That is, the doors were open, but the place didn't appear to be open for business. Inside he found Sheriff Gage standing at the bar, holding a cup of coffee. Behind the bar was a man wearing an apron. Although Clint had been in the saloon yesterday, he had not seen this particular bartender before.

The man was just under six feet, dark-haired, probably in his mid to late twenties. His face was not pale, but neither was it tanned. It had the look of a face that had been tan at one time but was beginning to lose it. Clint deduced that the man had at one time spent time outside, but had been inside for quite a while—probably as a bartender.

He looked around as he walked to the bar, but there was no one else in the place.

"Sheriff," he said, with a nod.

"Coffee?" Gage asked.

"Sure."

The bartender went and poured a cup of coffee and brought it over to Clint.

"Well, where's this fellow you wanted me to meet?" Clint asked, holding the cup.

"Right here," Gage said, inclining his head toward the bartender.

Clint looked at the bartender and found the man looking back at him with a puzzled expression.

"What?" Clint asked. "A bartender?"

"What's goin' on?" the bartender asked. "Sheriff?"

"Gil," Gage said, "I want you to meet Clint Adams, the Gunsmith."

"I know who Adams is," the man called Gil said, looking annoyed now rather than puzzled.

"Clint," the sheriff went on with the introductions, "meet Gil Yates."

"Sheriff—" Clint said.

"Gage—" Gil Yates said.

"Gil," Gage said, ignoring both of them, "Adams here has taken on the job of transporting that prison wagon to Huntsville Prison."

"I heard about that," Yates said, idly wiping the bar top with a dirty rag. "The deputy got hurt, right?"

"Right," Gage said. "Shot, to be exact."

"So, what's that got to do with me?"

"Adams, here, needs somebody to ride shotgun."

"I'll ask you again, Gage," Yates said, "what's that got to do with me?"

Gage put his coffee down and turned to face Yates.

"Ain't you been tellin' me that it's about time to be movin' on again?"

"So?"

"So, here's your chance."

"With him?" Yates asked. "I keep my ears open, Sheriff, I know who's in that wagon. Jeff Sawyer's men are not just gonna stand by and watch their leader go to prison."

"I know that," Gage said. "That's why Adams needs somebody to watch his back."

"And you're suggestin' me for the job?"

"I'm suggestin' that you volunteer for the job," Gage said.

"You're crazy."

"No," Gage said, "you're goin' crazy. You told me yourself."

"I just meant I was gettin' bored—"

"And does this sound borin' to you?"

"No," Yates said. "It sounds suicidal, though."

"Wait a minute," Clint said, cutting between both of them. "Before you start arguing about whether he should go or not, what qualifies him to do it?"

Gage looked at Clint and said, "Yates is about the best hand I ever saw with a gun, Adams."

Clint looked at the younger man, who looked away.

"What's he doing behind a bar, then?"

"Gil?" Gage said, looking at Yates.

Yates hesitated a moment, then said, "You're tellin' it, Sheriff. I got to go in the back for a little while."

Yates walked into the back room, and Gage looked at Clint again.

"Let's move to a table and I'll tell you a story," Gage said.

"Let's take the coffeepot," Clint said.

"I'll make it a short story."

"Let's take it anyway."

FIFTEEN

The story turned out to be a familiar one. As a young man, Gil Yates became fascinated with guns, and with the men who had reputations for using them. This led to him buying a gun early and learning how to use it. He became very good with it and eager to prove his ability. During his late teens and early twenties he killed several men in gunfights.

"I don't know how many," Gage said. "I don't think he even kept count."

"That's in his favor, anyway," Clint said.

Yates's story was very similar to his own. He had been forced to kill men during his early years of carrying a gun, because that was a hazard of wearing a pistol. Somebody always wanted you to prove you could use it. Clint, himself, had never kept count of the men he'd killed. All he knew was that it was too many.

"So what happened?" Clint asked. "What brought him here?"

"What brought him here was he was driftin'," Gage said. "What kept him here and put him behind that bar was a gunfight he didn't want any part of. He killed a kid, no more than sixteen, though he looked older. The gun he was wearin' made him look a lot older. The kid pushed Yates into a corner. Yates tried to talk him out of it, but the kid went for his gun and Yates killed him."

"And?"

"He hasn't worn his gun since. He's got a room out behind the saloon, and his gun is hangin' on a nail on the wall. He got a job as a bartender and that's where he's been, behind that bar for over a year."

"And you think he's ready to come out from behind the bar?"

"I know he is," Gage said. "He's been sayin' it for weeks."

Clint thought a moment before answering.

"Look, Gage, I appreciate that you're trying to do a good deed here—"

"Two good deeds," Gage said. "One for you, and one for him."

"That's fine," Clint said. "But if he hasn't used his gun in a year, how do you know he'll be any help to me?"

"You tell me," Gage said. "You know how to use a gun. Do you forget in a year?"

"No, you don't, but—"

"Look, Adams," Gage said, "there ain't a better man in town to back you up, and working on the side of the law is probably what he needs to get him started on the right path. It'd be a shame for him to leave here and fall into the same old ways, wouldn't it?"

Clint had to admit that it would.

"What's your interest?" he asked Gage.

"None, except that I've gotten pretty friendly with him. Well, that ain't so. Truth is, he don't talk much and ain't got any friends in town, but at least he talks to me, so I guess that makes me the closest thing to a friend he's got."

Clint thought a moment and then asked, "How good is he with a gun?"

"Real good."

"Fast?"

"I don't know how fast he is, but he hits what he shoots at. He was pretty fast that day against the kid, but . . ." Gage shrugged.

"Do you think he'll do it?"

"I think so," Gage said. "He's pretty damn bored behind that bar, and escortin' Jeff Sawyer to prison, that's pretty strong stuff for a young man."

"How old is he?"

"Twenty-five, I think."

"Not so young."

"Not old, either," Gage said. "Younger than most."

"I guess."

They sat in silence for a while and then Gage asked, "What do ya say?"

"I'm willing to talk to him about it," Clint said. "I don't want him coming if you're pushing him into it."

"I'll talk to him," Gage said, standing up, "but he won't be talked into it. If he goes, it'll be because he wants to."

Clint watched Gage walk to the back and disappear through a door, then poured himself another cup of coffee.

SIXTEEN

When Gage entered the back storeroom, Yates was there. On top of a barrel lay his gun belt, coiled like a snake, and he was staring at it.

"Took it down off the nail, huh?" Gage asked.

Yates didn't turn and didn't register surprise that the sheriff was there. He continued to stare at the gun.

"Why are you doin' this?" he finally asked.

"Because it's a chance," Gage said, "a chance to get out from behind that bar, and a chance to get on the right side of the law."

"Adams is no lawman."

"No, but he's doin' a favor for one," Gage said. "He could have a badge, but he don't want one. That don't matter, though, Gil, does it?"

"No," Yates said, after a moment, "it don't."

"Does the job appeal to you?" Gage asked.

"Compared to what?" Yates asked, and then answered his own question. "Compared to day after day behind a bar? Yeah, it appeals to me. I just don't know. . . ."

"And you won't know, Gil," Gage said, "not

until you strap on that gun and see how it feels."

Gage watched while Yates continued to stare down at the gun belt. He watched as the younger man reached for the belt slowly, placed his hand on it for a few moments, then finally picked it up as if it weighed a hundred pounds and strapped it on.

"How does it feel?"

Yates turned around to face Gage.

"It's funny," he said, looking puzzled, "it feels like I never took it off."

"Why don't you go out and talk to Adams?" Gage said. "If you don't want the job, you don't have to take it."

"I know that."

"Go ahead," Gage said, standing aside, away from the doorway. "Listen to what he has to say."

"You talk him into wantin' me?" Yates asked.

"Whether he wants you to go along or not is up to him," Gage said. "I can't talk him into anythin' he don't want to do—same as you. You're both gonna have to make up your own minds about this."

Yates nodded, turned, and walked out of the room.

Clint looked up and saw Gil Yates walking toward him, wearing a gun. It was a worn Colt that had probably been his first gun, for the wooden grips were worn. As the younger man came closer, though, Clint noticed that the gun was clean and gleamed with oil. If the holster had stayed on a nail on the wall all these months, the gun had not. It had been cleaned, and probably cleaned again, and kept in proper working condition, even though it hadn't been used.

Clint was starting to think that maybe Gage had been right about Yates.

SEVENTEEN

"Mind if I sit?" Yates asked.

"Go ahead."

Yates sat across from Clint and stared at him.

"You really the Gunsmith?" Yates asked.

"I'm really Clint Adams," Clint said. "What other people call me is their business."

"I wanted to be known by a name once," Yates said. "You know, the somethin' kid, or somethin' like that."

"Did you ever come up with any?" Clint asked.

"No," Yates said, shaking his head. "Everything I came up with just sounded silly . . . and then the whole idea sounded silly."

"It is."

Yates nodded, and Clint waited for him to continue the conversation.

"Gage tells me you need help."

"I think so."

"Does the job pay?"

"No," Clint said, "at least, I don't think so. When we get to the other end you might be able to make a deal with somebody."

"You gettin' paid?"

Clint shook his head. "This is strictly a favor," he said.

"That deputy a friend of yours?"

Clint shook his head again. "I just met him yesterday."

"Then why are you doin' this?"

"I've been asking myself the same question."

"And?"

"I guess I get bored," Clint said. "Or maybe I'm just a glutton for punishment. Or maybe I just don't know the answer . . . but you know what?"

"What?"

"I get the feeling you feel the same way," Clint said. "You're going to come with me, and you don't know why."

"I'm not sure why, it's true," Yates said, "but if you'll have me, I'd like to come along."

"Sure," Clint said, "why not? Can you be ready in an hour?"

"I'm ready now," Yates said. "I got nothin' to pack."

"I'll be back here within the hour, with the wagon. You got a horse?"

"Yeah, at the livery."

"That's it, then," Clint said, and extended his hand across the table. Yates took it.

"You know," Yates said, after releasing Clint's hand, "I always wanted to be like you."

Clint stood up and said, "I'm not somebody to be like, Gil, I'm somebody to be better than."

• • •

Clint hadn't seen Gage leave the saloon so when he saw the sheriff waiting out front he assumed that the saloon had a back door.

"So?" Gage asked.

"So what?"

"Is he goin' with you?"

"He is."

"That's great!"

"Gage," Clint said, regarding the man quizzically, "I still can't figure your angle."

"I don't have an angle."

"Do you just want to get Yates out of town?" Clint asked. "Is that it?"

"Sure I want to get him out of town," Gage said. "That's the point, ain't it?"

"Just because you like him."

"That's right."

Clint stared at Gage and then shook his head. Nothing in his previous dealings with the lawman—however few—had prepared him for this.

"Why you shakin' your head?" Gage asked.

"You just didn't strike me as the type when we met," Clint said. In fact, he still wasn't convinced that the sheriff was doing this purely out of concern for Gil Yates.

"What type?" Gage asked, with a frown.

"The type who wanted to help other people."

Gage looked hurt. "What did I do to make you think that?" he asked. "I want to help lots of people."

"Just not me, right?"

"I am helpin' you by gettin' you Yates," Gage reminded him.

"That's right, you are," Clint said, "and you can help me some more by getting those prisoners ready."

"They'll be ready."

Gage turned and headed across the street to the jail. The man had his own reasons for doing what he was doing, and Clint decided that maybe he just wasn't going to find out what they were.

He turned and walked the other way, toward the livery. It was time to retrieve the prison wagon and get this trip under way.

EIGHTEEN

"You're what?"

"I'm leavin' town, Lauren," Gil Yates said.

"When?"

"Today."

She stared at Yates in disbelief.

"Just like that?"

Yates spread his arms in a helpless gesture.

"The chance came up, Lauren," Yates said, "and I've got to take it."

"But, Gil—"

"Lauren," Yates said, "you knew I was gonna leave soon."

"Yes, but . . . not this soon."

"What are you talkin' about?" Yates asked. "It's been months."

Lauren was a tall blonde in her thirties, ten years older than Gil Yates. She was a big, full-bodied woman with whom Yates had been exchanging hot glances for the first six months he'd been in town. It was not until the last six months that they had become involved.

She moved closer to him, pressing her full

breasts against his chest.

"Gil, baby, we wasted so much time when you first came to town."

She took hold of his right hand and moved it to her mouth. She sucked on his index finger, then moved the hand down over her body. He could feel the nipples of her big breasts right through her dress. She took his hand further down still, to her thighs and then beneath her dress. Her flesh was hot to the touch, and when she brought his hand between her legs it was like a furnace. Usually, when she was expecting him, she didn't wear underwear, and he was used to feeling her wiry pubic hair and then her wet vagina. This time, however, she hadn't been expecting him and was wearing underwear. Still, he could feel her heat and wetness right though the cotton. He rubbed his hand over her and she shuddered.

"Oh, Gil . . ."

"I'm sorry, honey," Yates said, easing his hand from between her legs. He was rigid and ready himself, but he had promised Clint Adams that he'd be ready to leave. "I have to go."

"You son of a bitch, Gil!" she hissed. She was flushed, and he could smell her readiness. She grabbed the front of his shirt savagely. "You're leaving me with him! What will I do . . . how will I . . . Jesus, Gil, I can't . . ."

"Oh, hell . . ." he said thickly. He reached between her legs again and tore off her underwear. Quickly, he unbuckled his pants and dropped them, then slid his hands beneath her buttocks

and lifted her up. She was heavy, but he was able
to handle her weight and slid her down onto him.
As his penis entered her, her eyes widened and she
hissed, letting air out slowly between her teeth.

He turned and pinned her back to the wall and
then began to move, sliding her up and down
him. He could feel her wetness on his thighs
and on his hands as he continued to cradle her
ass cheeks in his hands.

"God . . ." she said, putting her arms around
him, bringing her legs up to hold him tightly.
"Gil . . . God . . . Gil . . ." she kept saying, over
and over while he lunged into her, slamming her
against the wall. Her head hit the wall once, but
she didn't notice because she was already dizzy.

As in many times in the past her husband could
have walked in on them at any minute, but that
had always been part of the appeal for them.

She began to pant and claw at him and suddenly he felt her tremble. He quickly covered her
mouth with his to muffle the scream he knew
was coming, and when it came he erupted inside
of her and moaned back into her open mouth. . . .

Gil Yates stopped at the back door and turned
to look at Lauren. She was on her knees, her dress
hiked up around her hips. Her blond hair was
tousled, her lips swollen, and she still smelled
heavily of sex. Every instinct in him wanted to
go back to her and take her again, this time on
the floor. He'd never met a woman with the sex-
ual appetite of Lauren before. He might have left

town a lot sooner were it not for her. It was time now, though, and he couldn't allow the woman to keep him there, not when it was clearly time to go.

He'd been playing with fire for months now, and it was probably a good idea that he was leaving town.

The last time, he told himself as he opened the door, the very last time I get involved with the town sheriff's wife.

He took one last look at Lauren Gage, her eyes glazed, her breasts heaving, and then went out the door.

Sheriff Calvin Gage watched from a doorway across the street as Gil Yates left his house by the back door. Gage had discovered what was going on between his wife and Yates only a month before. He chose to believe that he had caught it in the beginning, and did not want to think about how long it might actually have been going—like since the day Yates had first come to town!

He had not approached either of them with his knowledge. He chose, instead, to wait until he could take his revenge on Gil Yates without any reprisals. He was the law, after all, so it wouldn't look good for him to just gun the man down. Besides, there was no way he could have stood up to Yates with a gun. Instead, he chose to use his superior intelligence.

When Clint Adams came to town with a prison wagon bearing Jeff Sawyer, Gage saw his chance.

He knew Yates was becoming bored, but he didn't want the man riding out free and clear, not after what had been going on between him and Lauren.

This, then, was the perfect solution. Not even Clint Adams was going to be able to get Jeff Sawyer and those others to Huntsville, not with Sawyer's gang on his trail. Adams was going to get killed doing his favor, and now—to Calvin Gage's satisfaction—Gil Yates would get killed along with him.

As for Lauren . . . well, Gage would take care of her in his own time. After all, she wasn't going anywhere.

He turned and walked back to his office to get Sawyer and the other two ready.

NINETEEN

Once the team was hooked up to the prison wagon, Clint stowed his supplies beneath the seat and then saddled Duke. He had decided to take the big gelding along, preferring not to have to return to town after the prisoners were delivered to Huntsville.

He tied Duke loosely to the back of the wagon, then climbed atop and drove it out of the livery and over to the saloon. When he got there Gil Yates was sitting astride a handsome roan which may or may not have been a gelding. He didn't know where Yates had been keeping his horse, because he hadn't seen the man or the animal at the livery.

"Good-looking animal," Clint said.

"Thanks."

"Gelded?"

"Yup."

Clint stepped down from the wagon and looked the animal over.

"What is he, about four?"

"Exactly," Yates said. "You know your horses—but then you would."

71

Yates rode his horse around behind the wagon so he could get a clear look at Duke. His roan might have matched up with the big black in conformation, but in sheer size Duke was a clear winner.

"That's a powerful animal," Yates said. "Nine?"

"Yes."

"Gettin' up there."

"Aren't we all?" Clint asked. "Are you ready to go?"

"I'm ready."

"Let's get over to the jail," Clint said. "The sheriff should be ready to give the prisoners up."

Clint climbed atop the wagon again and headed over to the jail with Gil Yates riding alongside.

"The roan have a name?" Clint asked.

"I call him Lincoln."

Clint looked over at Yates, who was staring straight ahead. He decided not to ask.

When they reached the jail, Calvin Gage stepped outside to greet them.

"Our boys ready to go, Sheriff?" Clint asked, climbing down.

"They're ready."

Yates dismounted and followed both men inside.

Gage took the keys off a wooden peg and turned to Clint.

"Want to open the wagon?"

Clint turned and gave the key to Yates.

"Open 'er up, Gil."

"Right."

Yates went outside, and Clint went into the back with Gage.

"Gentlemen," Gage announced, "your carriage is here."

"Hey, Adams," Sawyer said, standing up from his cot, "ready to die, huh?"

"Shut up, Sawyer," Gage said. "Step back from the door."

Clint heard something behind him and turned. Yates was standing there holding leg irons.

"Thought you might need these."

"Right," Clint said. "Thanks."

He took one set from Yates and tossed them into Sawyer's cell when Gage opened the door. He instructed Sawyer to snap them on himself, then did the same with the other two prisoners. That done, he, Gage, and Yates marched—or shuffled—them out to the wagon and watched as they struggled with the single step to get inside. Once they were inside, Yates closed the door and locked it.

"Hey, kid," Sawyer called, "who are you?"

Yates didn't answer.

"Got yourself some help, huh, Adams?" Sawyer asked. "This kid know that he signed up to die?"

"Why don't you ask him?"

Sawyer looked at Yates.

"You know who I am?"

"I know who you are, Sawyer."

"You do?"

"Uh-huh."

"Then what the hell are you doin' here?" Sawyer asked. "You must know that you ain't gettin' me to Huntsville—not even close enough to smell it."

"We'll see," Yates said, and walked away.

"Hope you can use that iron on your hip, friend," Sawyer called out to Yates, "'cause you're gonna need it."

Yates walked away from the wagon and stood next to Gage.

"Sorry to see you go, Gil," Gage said.

Yates looked at the sheriff and wondered for the hundredth time if the man knew about him and Lauren.

"Are you?"

"Sure," Gage said. "Ain't that many people around this town I can just talk to, ya know?"

"Sure," Yates said. "You know, I could get killed doin' this."

"Yeah," the sheriff said, "I know."

Yates looked at Gage, who was looking away at the wagon. Just for a moment Yates wondered if that was the idea. If Gage knew about him and Lauren, maybe that was why he'd introduced him to Clint Adams. He probably figured that whoever was trying to get Sawyer to Huntsville was going to end up dead. It was a good way to get somebody else to do your dirty work for you.

If the man knew.

"Gage—"

"Listen, Gil," Gage said, cutting the man off. He turned and faced Yates. "If you catch a bullet, no hard feelings, huh?"

Before Yates could reply, Gage walked away.

"What's going on?" Clint asked.

Yates looked at Clint and said, "Nothing. Just sayin' good-bye."

"Oh yeah?" To Clint it looked like something else, but he kept his mouth shut about it.

"We ready to go?" Yates asked.

"Yeah," Clint said. "I forgot to ask you something."

"Yeah?"

"Can you handle a rig like this?"

"Yeah, I can."

"I think we should take turns driving it. Any objections?"

"None."

"I'll start, then, and you ride along."

"Fine."

"Uh, Yates, Sawyer's probably going to keep trying to get under your skin."

"I've been tending bar for the past year," Yates said. "People are always tryin' to get under your skin when you're a bartender."

Clint smiled.

"Yeah, I guess so. Let's get going."

Clint climbed aboard the wagon, released the brake, and called out to the team while flicking the reins.

They rode to the north end of town.

"Hey, boys," Sawyer called, "we're gettin' a pretty good send-off."

"Look at her," Reggie Prince said.

Clint looked and saw that they were passing a small house with a very attractive blond woman standing on the porch. She was leaning against a wooden post, a decidedly sexy pose, considering her dress was ruffled and her hair was mussed.

"Jesus," Mark Lacy said, "she looks like she just got out of bed."

The woman was watching them—or one of them.

Clint turned and stared at Yates, who was looking at the woman. Suddenly, as if he could feel Clint watching him, Yates turned and looked back.

"Friend of yours?" Clint asked.

"That," Gil Yates said, "is the sheriff's wife."

Clint frowned, and Yates looked away, but not at the woman.

Yep, Clint decided, there was definitely something going on in Culpepper that he didn't want to know about.

TWENTY

Just as Clint had predicted, when Yates took his shift on the wagon Sawyer started talking his ear off. First he tried to scare Yates with threats of what his gang would do to him, and then he tried to buy him off with promises of large sums of money. Clint had to give Yates credit, he managed to remain silent throughout.

They pushed through the whole day without stopping, taking some water and jerky for lunch. When they did camp Clint announced that it would be a cold camp, water and jerky again.

"We don't know where Sawyer's gang is," Clint explained, "and we don't want to go announcing our location."

"No need to explain," Yates said. "I understand about a cold camp."

Clint walked to the wagon and tossed in a few pieces of beef jerky and a canteen of water.

"At least in that jail cell we got hot food," Sawyer said.

"I hope you enjoyed it," Clint said. "It might be the last hot food you get."

"I doubt it," Sawyer said, with a laugh. "Even if I do hang, the condemned man always gets a hearty meal. I'll have all my favorites."

"Don't worry," Clint said, "you'll get your opportunity."

"Not a chance."

Clint went back to where Yates was and sat across from him.

"You did well today," Clint said.

"What does it take to drive a wagon?"

"No, I meant keeping quiet and letting Sawyer run on at the mouth."

"Oh, that," Yates said. "Why not let him talk? He's due to get his neck stretched, ain't he?"

"It doesn't bother you?"

"No."

"What about all that talk about money?"

"You can believe what you want, Clint," Yates said, "but I ain't interested in money."

"Not even lots of it?"

Yates stared at Clint.

"I've seen what lots of money can do to people, Clint," he said, "firsthand. I don't want it. I'm happy with enough in my pocket to buy a meal, a drink, and either a woman, or a handful of poker chips."

"Sounds like a simple life."

"It is," Yates said, "or it will be, once we get this job over with."

"A couple of days should do it."

"A couple of days from here to Huntsville?" Yates asked. "How do you figure that?"

Clint chewed the jerky in his mouth and swallowed before answering.

"We're going to travel at night."

"Isn't that dangerous?"

"We'll be on a road," Clint said.

"Isn't *that* dangerous with Sawyer's gang lookin' for us?"

"Look," Clint said, "by day we stay off the road, by night on it."

"You don't think they'll travel at night?"

"I don't think they'll think they have to," Clint said. "They're probably as arrogant as he is. They don't think there's a chance that we'll make it."

"And we do?"

"Yeah," Clint said, "we do."

"You're tellin' me you wouldn't have taken this job on if you didn't think you could deliver them?"

"That's right."

Yates stared at Clint for a few moments.

"I can't tell if you're bein' truthful or not."

"You want me to tell you?"

"No," Yates said, "that's okay."

Later they sat on the ground across from each other, each wrapped in a blanket and watching the stars. It was too dark to watch anything else, because the moon was hidden behind a patch of clouds.

"I have a deck of cards," Yates said.

"Too dark."

"It's been a long time since I slept on the ground."

"A sky like this," Clint said, "is a small price to pay for a sore butt in the morning."

"I'll try to remember that," Yates said.

"I'll take the first watch and wake you in three hours," Clint said. "I want to get an early start, before daylight, and then the rest of the way we'll push through at night."

"Maybe the moon'll come up clearer tomorrow night," Yates said.

"That would help," Clint said. "Traveling at night is going to be hazardous, and some extra light would make it easier."

"Sure you don't want me to take the first watch?" Yates asked.

"I've got it," Clint said. "Get some sleep. You're going to need it once we start pushing hard."

TWENTY-ONE

When Yates shook Clint the next morning he came immediately awake. He looked around and saw that it was still pretty dark.

"First light's still a ways away," Yates said, "but thought you'd want to get started."

"You thought right," Clint said.

Hitching up the team awoke the three prisoners, who complained about it. Clint and Yates both ignored them.

"You know," Sawyer said, "they're plannin' to hang me when I get to Huntsville. If that happens I'd at least like to have some conversation between now and then."

"Have it with your fellow prisoners," Clint said. "You won't get any conversation from us."

"That go for you, too, kid?" Sawyer asked.

Yates didn't even look at him.

"I guess that's my answer," Sawyer said. He turned and looked at Lacy and Prince. "I guess that just leaves me with you fellas, huh?"

Prince scowled, but Lacy said, "I'll talk to you,

Sawyer, if you get me out of here."

Sawyer just glared at the man in annoyance and then turned his head so he could watch Clint and Yates saddle their horses. He felt if he watched them constantly he might spot a weakness in one or the other that he could put to his use.

He knew the reputation of Clint Adams, but he had a rep of his own to live up to. He couldn't afford to be intimidated by someone else's.

As for the kid, he didn't know him from Adam— or Adams. He laughed at his own joke and wrote the kid off. The man to concentrate on was Clint Adams, so he watched the man's every move very carefully.

Jeff Sawyer had not gotten to where he was without knowing his enemies.

The joke was on him that time, and he didn't even notice it.

Yates took the first shift on the prison wagon, and Clint took his turn after midday.

"You fellas still have time to change your minds, you know," Sawyer said loudly. He couldn't see Clint, but speaking out the side that way he knew he could be heard. "There'd be lots of money in it for you, Adams, if you let me go."

"And us!" Lacy said anxiously.

"Shut up, damn it!" Clint heard Sawyer snap. "You're gonna serve five years, for Chrissake. I'm headin' for a rope!"

It sounded to Clint like Sawyer might just be

coming to the end of his rope. He was starting to sound agitated, like maybe he wasn't so sure that his men were going to set him free in time.

"Don't say another word!" Clint heard Sawyer say to Lacy. He knew he wasn't talking to Reggie Prince because the black man hardly spoke.

"Adams, can you hear me?"

Clint didn't answer.

"I know you can hear me, you son of a bitch. I'm gonna keep talkin' at you day in and day out and I ain't gonna stop."

"It's your breath," Clint said to himself.

Yep, Jeff Sawyer was starting to get real worried, and as he kept silent Clint knew that the man would just get worse and worse until he was faced with that rope.

Sawyer continued to talk through the afternoon, and Clint just kept on ignoring the man. Finally, Sawyer stopped, and Clint thought that it must surely be because of a sore throat.

It was not a sore throat, however. It was the touch of Reggie Prince's hand on his shoulder that stopped Sawyer from talking. He turned to say something in anger and stopped when he saw the black man holding his finger to his lips.

"What?" Sawyer whispered.

Prince beckoned to Sawyer, who joined the man at the back of the wagon.

"Look," Prince said, pointing out the barred window.

Sawyer looked impatiently, saying, "What the hell—"

"Just look carefully," Prince said, his mouth close to Sawyer's ear.

"What's goin'—" Lacy started to ask, but both of the other men waved him silent.

"I see it," Sawyer said finally. Off in the distance there was a cloud of dust, the kind that could only be raised by a bunch of riders.

Now the question remained, who were they and were they headed in this direction?"

"Are those your men?" Lacy whispered from right behind Sawyer.

Sawyer looked at him and said, "Time will tell."

For the rest of the afternoon the three men in the wagon were silent, watching the dust cloud in the distance, willing it to get closer and closer.

It was the inexperience of Gil Yates that kept him from seeing the cloud of dust. He had not been on the trail in more than a year and those kinds of senses tended to rust somewhat when not in use. When they changed places again that evening, it was just light enough for Clint to see the cloud when he turned in his saddle.

"Gil!"

"Yeah?"

"How long has that been there?" Clint asked, pointing behind them.

Yates turned to look at Clint and reined in the

team so he could look behind them.

"What?" he asked.

"That cloud of dust."

Yates narrowed his eyes and peered into the distance behind them.

"Oh, shit," he said, hanging his head. He looked at Clint and said, "I'm sorry, Clint. I'm a bit rusty after a year behind a bar."

"Yeah," Clint said, knowing he couldn't fully blame Yates. He should have been looking behind them himself, knowing that Yates hadn't been on the trail in over a year's time. "It's my fault."

"Well, do you think it's them?"

"I don't know," Clint said. "I guess we can hope it's not."

"It's them," Sawyer called out. "Take my word for it, Adams. My boys will be on you by noon tomorrow."

"You better hope they're not," Clint said.

"Or what? You'll shoot me down in cold blood? You ain't the type."

"Maybe he's not," Yates said. "Then again, maybe I am." That seemed to shut Sawyer up. Whatever he knew about Clint, he knew next to nothing about Gil Yates—which meant he didn't know if Yates was capable of a cold blooded shooting.

"Whether it's them or not we'd better keep moving," Clint said.

"Maybe," Yates said, "I should ride back there and find out."

Clint frowned a moment. It was a good idea, only he thought he was more qualified to ride back and look. The only problem with that was he also thought he was better qualified to stay with the prisoners.

Finally, he decided that staying with the prison wagon was his reponsibility.

"Okay," he said to Yates, "but just take a look. Make sure they don't get a look at you. Got it?"

"I got it," Yates said.

As Yates dropped down from the wagon, untied his horse, and mounted up, Sawyer spoke up.

"How are you going to know they're my men?" he asked Clint and Yates.

Yates looked at Clint.

"We're not," Clint said, "but we'll react the same way, whoever it is. We'll avoid them."

"But I can tell you how to tell if it's them," Sawyer said. "Then you'll know for sure."

"Why would you do that?" Clint asked.

"Because," Sawyer said, "I want you to know it's them. I want you to see what you're gonna be up against."

Yates looked at Clint again, who simply shrugged.

"If he wants to help us, we'll let him," Clint said. He looked at Sawyer and said, "How do we know it's them?"

"The leader," Sawyer said, "will have hair so blond it looks almost white. Also, one other man will be very big, nearly six-and-a-half feet tall.

You won't be able to miss him, because he rides a white horse."

Yates looked at Clint and said, "It sounds too easy."

"He's got no reason to lie," Clint said. "He wants us to be scared."

"If it's them," Sawyer said, "there'll be a baker's dozen of them. That's somethin' to be afraid of, considerin' there's only two of you."

Yates looked at Clint and said, "Good point."

"Do you want me to do it?"

"No," Yates said, "I'll do it."

"Remember what I said," Clint reminded him. "A quick look and then back here."

"I heard you."

Before Yates left, Clint briefly explained to him what the next three towns would be, and that he would keep the wagon due north of these towns, but would not enter any of them.

"If you think you've lost us," he went on, "just ride through one of the towns and continue north."

"All right."

"Chances are I'll camp for the night, because I don't want to risk traveling at night alone, and I'll be keeping a cold camp."

Yates nodded his understanding.

"If you come up on us, sing out before you ride in so I don't shoot you."

"I'll remember that," Yates said firmly.

Clint shook hands with the younger man and said, "Good luck."

"Thanks."

Yates started to take his hand back, but Clint held it fast.

"If you don't catch up by tomorrow night, I'm going to assume you're not coming."

"Are you thinkin' that I might just keep ridin'?"

Clint released his hand and said, "For whatever reason, I'll assume that you're not coming."

Yates stared at Clint a moment, then nodded his understanding and rode off.

As Yates rode off, Clint dismounted, tied Duke to the wagon, and climbed into the seat.

"The time when you'll have to deal with my men is getting closer, Adams," Sawyer said.

"So is the time that you'll arrive at Huntsville, Sawyer," Clint said. "Once we get you there, I think your men will forget about you."

"You ain't gettin' me there."

"We'll see about that," Clint asked, "won't we?"

"Oh yeah," Sawyer agreed, "we'll definitely see about that."

As the wagon got back under way Mark Lacy asked Sawyer, "Why did you tell them what your men look like?"

"I explained that to them," Sawyer said. "Weren't you listenin'?"

"I didn't understand."

Sawyer looked at Prince.

"You understand, Reggie?"

"Yeah," Prince said, "I understand, Sawyer."

"Then explain it to this idiot, will you?"

Prince looked at Lacy and said, "He just playin' with their minds, Lacy. He want them to know how many men is after them, and he want them to know they gettin' closer. He want them to be scared!"

"That's Clint Adams out there," Lacy pointed out. "You think he's gonna be scared?"

"If he's not scared," Sawyer said, "he's gonna be careful, and bein' careful can get you just as killed."

"I still don't get it," Lacy said, shaking his head.

Prince looked away, and Sawyer did, too, saying, "Luckily, you don't have to."

TWENTY-TWO

Billy July wondered why he was out here, riding all the hell over Texas with twelve other men, trying to find the prison wagon that was taking Jeff Sawyer to Huntsville to face a rope. Hadn't he been wanting to take over the Sawyer gang for months now? Didn't he think that he could be a better leader than Jeff Sawyer ever was?

And there was his answer, staring him in the face. The other twelve men with him—most of them, anyway—thought that Sawyer was the best leader they'd ever had. Now, however, they were following Billy July to try to free Sawyer. If they succeeded in busting Sawyer loose, Billy July was going to look pretty good, and he might be able to build up some support from some of the others in the gang for when he wanted to take over.

If they didn't succeed . . . well, July thought that he would come out looking okay then, too, just for having spent all this time try-ing.

One way or the other, this would work to July's advantage.

• • •

Using the cloud of dust as a reference point, Gil Yates rode back the way they had come. He urged his horse into a gallop and had to admit that he liked the way it felt. He had not ridden his horse in earnest the whole time he was living in Culpepper. He could feel that the horse was enjoying this, as well. But he wasn't out here to enjoy himself.

He rode for several hours before he realized that he was almost upon them. As he had closed ground on them, the cloud of dust had become less defined. Looking around he found a high ground vantage point where he could take cover behind a stand of trees and brush and get a look at the group as they went by. He rode his horse up the hill, mentally estimating how far behind the wagon the group was. If he had ridden for three hours it was safe to assume that they were about six hours behind the wagon—that is, if they were riding at the same pace he was, which they probably were not. In any case, it meant that he was about six hours behind the prison wagon now.

He dismounted and tied Lincoln loosely to a tree. He then took up a position from where he'd be able to see the men as they rode by. He wondered how he was going to get back ahead of the group to tell Clint what he had learned without them seeing him. If he had to circle around them, that was going to add time to his trip back.

He stopped wondering as the men came into view. They were not riding at the same fast pace he had been, but neither were they riding at a leisurely pace. As long as they continued on at that pace, he'd be able to get ahead of them.

He took cover behind a bush and peered carefully at the men as they passed him. He was far enough away from them so they wouldn't see him, but near enough so that he could see them to make out the men Sawyer had described to him.

And they were easy to make out.

First, the big man on the white horse stood out, and probably would have stood out even without the horse. He was easily the largest man Yates had ever seen, and he dwarfed the horse beneath him. The white horse was the only one in the bunch, who numbered thirteen by Yates's count.

Riding at the head of the group was the blond-haired man Sawyer had spoken of. Yates could clearly see that the man's hair beneath his hat was almost white.

These were indeed Jeff Sawyer's men, and there were thirteen of them.

Thirteen against two.

Suddenly, the job back at the saloon didn't look so bad to Gil Yates.

"Hey, Billy?"

July turned and saw Tally Turner riding up next to him. Turner was the same age as July, thirty-five, and they had known each other longer than any other two men in the gang. They were the first two to ever ride with Sawyer.

"What is it?" July asked.

"I got a feelin'," Turner said.

"What kind of feeling?"

"I don't know," Turner said, moving his shoulders. "Like maybe we're bein' watched?"

"You see anybody?" July asked, without looking around.

"Well, no—"

"Anybody else see anybody?"

"No—well, I ain't asked—"

"Well, ask," July said, "and do it without any fuss. Let me know what you find out."

"Okay."

Turner took his horse back and once again July was riding at the head of the group alone, just like a leader should.

TWENTY-THREE

Yates waited until the thirteen were well past him before remounting. He couldn't ride back the way he'd come. He was going to have to cut a wide loop around the men, get ahead of them, and then try to catch up with Clint. He wanted to do it by nightfall. He thought Clint should know as soon as possible that there were thirteen men on their trail.

He mounted up and rode west a ways, then reined in when he figured it was time to ride north again. He hesitated, though, remembering what Clint Adams had said to him. If he wasn't back by the next night, Clint would conclude that he wasn't coming back . . . for whatever reason.

Was Clint telling him that it was all right with him if he decided to just keep going and deal himself out of what looked like a losing hand? And even if it was all right with Clint, was it all right with him?

No, he couldn't do that. The man he once was wouldn't do that. He had told Clint that he'd help him, and he had to keep his word. At the very least, if he wanted out, he'd have to ride back to Clint, tell him about the thirteen men, and then deal himself out—if that's what he wanted to do.

After all, two against thirteen . . .

Well, he had plenty of time to make up his mind. He nudged his horse's ribs and started riding north at a gallop.

"He ain't comin' back, Adams," Jeff Sawyer said again. He'd been saying the same thing for most of the afternoon into the early evening.

"That young fella has decided to believe what I been tellin' him," the man went on. "That's what you should do, Adams. Believe me."

Clint didn't answer.

"Look, just leave the door open when you camp tonight. I don't even want a horse . . . or a gun. My boys'll find me soon enough."

"And what then?" Clint asked.

There was a long silence, as if Sawyer hadn't been ready for Clint to answer him.

"What do you mean, what then?"

"Are you just going to forget that I tried to take you to Huntsville?" Clint asked. "Aren't you and your boys going to come after me?"

"Naw," Sawyer said, "I wouldn't do that to you, not after you let me go." The man's tone was as innocent as he could make it.

"And what about the deputy?"

There was a pause and then Sawyer said in a totally different voice, "What about him?"

"Aren't you going to go back to Culpepper to finish him off?"

"What for?"

"Come on, Sawyer," Clint said. "I'm not stupid, and I don't think you are. If I let you go, you'll get your revenge on me and the deputy— especially him, since he's the one who brought you in."

There was another period of silence. Clint knew the man was thinking about his answer carefully.

"Okay," Sawyer said finally, "maybe I will go after the deputy. After all, if he finds out I got away he'll just come after me again."

"Can you blame him? After what you did to his wife?"

"I didn't do nothin' to his wife," Sawyer said.

"You're denying that you and your men were at the deputy's ranch?"

"No, I ain't denying it," Sawyer said, "but I didn't touch his wife. It was the others, my men. They done it. I didn't lay a hand on her."

Clint didn't reply. Even if the man was telling the truth, he had taken his men there and then stood by and watched.

"So maybe I will go after him," Sawyer said, "but that'd be self-defense. I wouldn't have no reason to go after you, though."

Clint remained silent.

"So what do ya say, Adams?" Sawyer asked. His tone was now touched with a degree of hope. "Just leave the door open and I'll sneak away in the night. You'll never hear from me again."

Clint stayed quiet.

"Adams?"

Quiet.

"Adams! What the hell—" Sawyer stopped, just as his voice was becoming strident. "Oh, I see what you're doin'," he said, after a few moments. "Teasin' me, huh? Havin' some fun?"

Clint didn't answer.

"Well, that's a mistake, Adams, a big mistake. Now when my men catch up and set me free, I'm gonna see to it that you die real slow. Real slow!"

"Now that's about what I'd expect from you," Clint said, more to himself than to Sawyer.

TWENTY-FOUR

Billy July reined his horse in when Tally Turner came riding up beside him again.

"What'd you find out?" he asked Turner.

"Nobody saw nothin', for sure."

"What do you mean, for sure?"

"Well, Kendall thinks he might've seen a man in some trees."

"Doin' what?"

"Nothin'."

"Nothin'? You mean, like watchin' us? Maybe countin' how many men we got?"

"I mean—"

"Goddamn it," July said. "Why didn't he speak up sooner?"

"He didn't think nothin' of it until I started askin'," Turner said.

"Stupid ass," July said.

Turner winced and said, "I wouldn't let him hear you call him that, Billy."

They both turned and looked back at the six and a half foot tall Kendall Rhodes.

"He's as dumb as he is big," July said. "Besides,

he knows I'm the leader of this outfit now."

"Well, yeah, until we break Sawyer loose."

"Right," July said, "until then."

"What do ya wanna do?"

July heaved a sigh and said, "Take two men and go back and check it out, then catch up with us."

"Right."

"And don't take too long."

"Okay, Billy."

"Tally?"

"Yeah?"

"Take Kendall with you."

Turner swallowed, but said, "Okay."

Most of the men in the gang were afraid of the big man, because of his size, and his temper, but it was true that he wasn't very smart, and more often than not a fast talker could get the best of him.

Billy July was a fast talker, and he was the most educated of the gang.

Turner was neither, so he usually just kept quiet around Kendall.

Turner, Kendall, and one other man rode back the way they had come, while July kept going with the other nine men.

He knew that Turner and Kendall would be loyal to Sawyer, but he felt he had a better than fifty-fifty chance of winning the loyalty of the other men. Once the Sawyer Gang became the July Gang, they would write a new chapter in the history of the American West.

• • •

Tally Turner was confused.

On one hand, he felt friendship for Billy July. On the other hand, he was loyal to Jeff Sawyer. Turner had been in many gangs in his lifetime, but none had ever been as successful as the Sawyer Gang. He'd never followed a leader with such loyalty as he followed Jeff Sawyer.

So what was he to do now that he knew Billy July wanted to take over the gang? Be loyal to his leader or his friend?

"Up there."

"What?" Turner asked, looking at Kendall.

"I said I thought I saw somebody up there on that hill," Kendall repeated.

"Oh," Turner said. "Well, let's go on up and take a look."

He, Kendall, and the other man, Dick Blevins, rode up the hill to the stand of trees and bushes and dismounted. Almost immediately Turner spotted where a horse had recently stood.

"One man," he said, looking around.

"Over here," Blevins said.

Turner walked over and saw the impression in the ground where a man had been kneeling.

"He was watching us through these bushes," Blevins said.

"Then I was right?" Kendall asked.

"You were right," Turner said.

The big man grinned, pleased with himself.

"Of course," Turner couldn't resist saying, "Billy wishes you'd said somethin' at the time."

"Oh," Kendall said, his usual blank look replacing the grin, "I guess I shoulda, huh?"

"I guess," Turner said. "Dick, look around, see what other sign you can find."

"Right."

"What should I do?" Kendall asked.

"Watch the horses."

"Right."

Both Blevins and Turner looked around but found no sign of any other horses or men.

"One man," Blevins said, "that's it."

"Lookin' us over," Turner said. "But why?"

"Why don't you let July worry about that?" Blevins said. "After all, he wants to be the big leader."

"Hey," Turner said, "he's been doin' okay since they locked up Jeff."

"Yeah," Kendall said, nodding his head, "real good."

Both men looked at Kendall and decided not to challenge his opinion.

They ignored it, but they wouldn't challenge it.

TWENTY-FIVE

Turner, Kendall, and Blevins caught up to the rest of the gang fairly quickly, and Turner fell in next to July to tell him what they had found.

"One man, that's all?" July asked.

"That's it," Turner said. "It looked like he just knelt there behind some bushes and watched us."

July scratched his cheek and thought a moment.

"We shot up that deputy and guard pretty good," he observed.

"It's a miracle the deputy got away from us," Turner said.

July gave him a sharp look. It was a sore point with July that the deputy had gotten away the way he did, and nobody had mentioned it up to now.

"We don't really know what kind of shape that deputy's in," July went on.

"At least we know for sure that guard's dead," Turner said. "We left him lying in the dust."

"Maybe the deputy made it to a town and got himself some help."

"And sent one man to check us out?"

"Maybe."

"It don't really matter, does it?" Turner asked. "I mean, unless he got hisself a whole posse to help him, we still outnumber him by a lot."

"He's a federal marshal," July said. "I doubt he'd put a posse together in some town. It's more likely he got patched up, picked up some supplies, and got going again."

"He's probably runnin' a cold camp, because we ain't even smelled nothin'," Turner said. "How the hell we gonna find them, Billy?"

"I don't know," July said. "We'll just have to keep riding."

Turner hesitated, then asked the question that was on his mind.

"You do *want* to find them, don't ya, Billy?"

July looked at him, then looked behind them to see how close the other men were.

"What do you mean by that?"

"Well, it ain't no secret that you wanna be the leader of this gang," Turner said.

"The others know that?"

"I know it," Turner said, "because we're friends."

"Uh-huh," July said. "Does that mean I'd have your support?"

"Heck, I don't know, Billy," Turner said. "If we break Sawyer out, it is his gang, ya know?"

"For now," July said.

"Billy, why you wanna be the leader anyway?" Turner asked.

"Because," July said, "I'm smarter than Sawyer, and more ambitious. With me as leader, Tally, this gang will make a lot more money. You know, all I need is one man to back me up, and the rest will fall in line."

"It would be easier for you if we didn't free Sawyer, wouldn't it?"

"That would be the easy way," July said, wording his reply carefully, "but I'd rather win leadership with him free, Tally. If I do that, then I'll be a true leader. Understand?"

"Sure, Billy," Turner said, "I understand. That means you do want to find that wagon and set him free, right?"

"Of course I do, Tally," July said, keeping his face front so that Turner couldn't see his eyes, "of course I do."

Turner heaved a sign of relief.

"Then how do we find them?" he asked.

"Like I said, Tally," July repeated, "we just keep riding."

"Texas is awful big, Billy."

July stroked his chin thoughtfully and said, "You're right, Tally. It is."

"You got an idea?"

"Yep," July said, "I just got an idea."

"What is it?"

"Well," July said, "I'll tell you . . ."

TWENTY-SIX

As darkness fell that night, Clint reined in the team, set the brake, and dropped down from the wagon's seat.

"We stoppin' for the night?" Sawyer asked.

"That's right."

"Can we get some hot food tonight?" Lacy asked.

"Nope," Clint said, loosing Duke's reins from the side of the wagon, "I'm running a cold camp again."

"Now where's the sense in that, Adams?" Sawyer asked. "My men are gonna find you anyway. You might as well make a fire and we can all have some hot food and coffee."

Clint grinned at the man and said, "Even if they are going to find us, Sawyer, why don't we just make them work for it a little, huh?"

"Hey," Sawyer said with a shrug, "it's up to you."

"That's right."

Clint unsaddled Duke and rubbed the big gelding down, then left him to graze. Next he undid the team and picketed them near Duke so they could also graze.

"Hey, Adams?" Sawyer called.

"What?" Clint asked. "You going to tell me again how your men are going to find us?"

"Naw," Sawyer said, "even I'm tired of hearing that."

"What is it, then?"

"We been cooped up in this wagon all day," Sawyer said. "You think we could get out so's we can, ya know, take care of business?"

"Don't you have some kind of pot in there?" Clint asked.

"Hell, no," Sawyer said, "that marshal used to let us out to do it."

"Hell," Clint said.

"Come on, Adams," Lacy said, "I'm about to bust."

"All right," Clint said, "but you're going to come out one at a time."

"Fine," Sawyer said, "just so long as we get out."

Clint moved around to the rear of the wagon and told them, "Step back from the door."

All three men moved back in the wagon.

"Who's first?" Clint asked.

"Go ahead, Lacy," Sawyer said. "You got the weakest bladder."

"What's that supposed to mean?" Lacy asked.

"It means you go first, Lacy," Clint said. He unlocked the door, then backed away and kept his hand on his gun. The gesture was just for show. He knew he'd be able to draw faster than any of the men could react, even without his hand on the gun butt. "Come on out."

He heard chains rattle as Lacy shuffled to the door, opened it, and stepped down.

"Oh, yeah," the man said, stretching, "that feels good in the legs."

"Move away from the wagon, Lacy."

The man obeyed.

"That's far enough."

Clint locked the door again, then turned to Lacy.

"Let's take a walk."

They walked at the pace allowed by Lacy's shackles, and Clint watched in distaste as the man emptied his bladder and his bowels.

"What do I use to clean up with?" Lacy asked.

"Grab some grass," Clint said.

"Jesus," Lacy said, and cleaned himself with a clump of grass.

Reggie Prince was next. Clint went through the same ritual with the black man, then walked him to a different spot and watched while he took care of his bodily functions.

Sawyer went last.

"You takin' me to the same spot they used?" the man asked.

"No," Clint said, "we'll go this way."

"Good," Sawyer said. "I don't like usin' the same outhouse as a nigger, if you know what I mean."

"I'm sure he'd appreciate that, Sawyer." Sawyer laughed.

"Shit," he said, "you tell him I said that he'd probably kill me."

"That would save the state a lot of trouble."

"You still think I'm gonna hang, don't you?" Sawyer asked, dropping his pants.

"You do, too, Sawyer," Clint said. "I can hear it in your voice."

"You don't hear nothin' in my voice I don't want you to hear, Adams, believe me."

"Yeah, right."

Sawyer bent way over, showing Clint his hairy, bare ass.

"Hey, Adams, my pants are stuck on these shackles. You wanna give me a hand?"

"Stop fooling around, Sawyer," Clint said.

Sawyer laughed and pulled up his pants, then turned to face Clint.

"I'm ready to go back."

"Let's go."

"Or maybe I'm ready to make a break for it," Sawyer said, with a crafty look.

"Go ahead," Clint said. "That would solve all of our problems."

"You'd like that, wouldn't you?" Sawyer asked. "Then you could put a bullet in my back."

"I've never shot a man in the back yet, Sawyer," Clint said, "but I'll bet I could make an exception in your case. Want to give it a try?"

The two men matched stares for a few moments, and then Sawyer shook his head.

"Naw," he said, "forget it. I wanna be around to see your face when my men catch up to us."

Clint walked him back to the wagon, unlocked the door, and watched as he struggled up the two steps back inside.

"How about some dinner?" Sawyer asked as Clint locked the door.

"Beef jerky coming up," Clint said.

TWENTY-SEVEN

Clint had to sleep with one eye open that night, since he didn't have Yates to split watches with. He couldn't stay awake all night because if he did he would fall asleep on the wagon the next day. He couldn't sleep soundly because somebody might come up on the camp or the prisoners might escape. What if he slept and they somehow got the door open?

Clint decided to move Duke over by him, hoping that the gelding would wake him if anything went wrong while he dozed.

It was the middle of the night when he suddenly felt Duke's muzzle bang into his shoulder. He'd been sleeping propped up against a tree, and the blow knocked him over and woke him up.

"What the hell—" he began, then stopped and listened.

Someone was approaching the camp. He reached up and patted Duke's nose with one hand and drew his gun with the other. He sat that way, waiting.

"Hello, the camp?" a voice called.

"Hello?"

"Clint?" the voice called. "It's me, Yates."

"Come on in," Clint called. It sounded like Yates, but he kept his gun ready anyway.

The moon was fuller this night than some of the others, so it was by moonlight that Clint was able to recognize Yates as the man walked into camp leading his horse. The roan looked completely worn-out, as did Yates, himself.

"You look like shit," Clint said, holstering his gun. "And so does your horse."

"I pushed it," Yates said. "I wanted to make sure I caught up with you tonight."

"You must've found something real important."

"Let's talk about it while I take care of Lincoln," Yates said.

Clint stood by and listened while Yates unsaddled his horse and rubbed him down.

"There's thirteen of them, Clint," Yates said.

"You recognized them?"

Yates nodded.

"Just like Sawyer said. One with white hair and a big man on a white horse."

"How far behind us are they?"

"Four or five hours, I figure—if they stopped to camp tonight."

"And they probably did," Clint said. "They have no reason to think they're this close behind us."

"We should keep movin'," Yates said.

"Your horse is half dead," Clint said. "He needs some rest, and so do you. We'll push through tomorrow night."

"Boy," Yates said, "I could sure use some hot coffee."

"I know," Clint said, "me, too, but if they're that close we don't dare risk it."

"I'll bet they're havin' some coffee."

"I'll bet they are."

Billy July drank his coffee while avoiding the flames of the camp fire. He didn't want to ruin his night vision, even though he wasn't going to be on watch tonight.

"What ya thinkin'?" Turner asked.

"Hmm?"

"What are you thinkin' so hard about?"

"Oh," July said, "I'm thinkin' about the future, Tally."

"What about it?"

"It's bright," July said, "that is, if we don't get killed tryin' to free Sawyer."

"Your plan should work, Billy," Turner said. "Instead of lookin' for that wagon we ride straight for Huntsville. If we don't run into them between here and there, maybe we'll get there before them and be there waiting for them."

"You like that plan, huh?"

Turner nodded.

"It's a damn good plan, Billy," he said. "Even the others think so."

"Well, that's real good," July said. "They agree with my plan. Kendall, too?"

"Well . . . yeah, him, too."

"Oh, that makes me feel a lot better," July said

sarcastically. "The dummy likes my plan."

"Billy—"

"If they'd listen to me without question, Tally," July said, "we'd be making money now, lots of it, instead of traipsing all over Texas."

Turner didn't know what to say to his friend, so he just remained quiet.

"I'll tell you something, Tally."

"What?"

"We're making one more try," July said, holding up one finger, "one more try to set him free, and then I'm done."

"What are you gonna do?"

"If they won't follow me after that," July said, "I'm leaving and I'll find my own gang. You can come or go, it's up to you."

"Billy—"

"I don't want to talk about it anymore, Tally," July said. "You go and set the watches with three men. I'm turning in. Let's get an early start for Huntsville in the morning."

"Okay, Billy," Turner said, standing up. "I'll wake you in the mornin'."

"Fine."

July rolled himself up in his blanket and tried to go to sleep, but his mind was racing with plans now. Plans for the future with *his* gang. Whether it was this gang or not was no longer of importance. What was important was that he would have his own gang, and he had to be ready with ideas to make money.

TWENTY-EIGHT

Clint woke Yates the next morning, having stood watch while the younger man got the rest he needed.

When Yates came awake he thought he smelled something.

"That's funny," he said. "I was dreamin' about coffee, and now I smell it."

"You do smell coffee," Clint said, and handed him a cup.

"And . . . beans?" Yates asked, sniffing the air.

"I decided to risk it, just to get something more than beef jerky into our stomachs," Clint said, handing Yates a plate of beans. "Drink up, and eat up. I've already put the fire out and we'll get going as soon as you're finished."

"Hey," Sawyer shouted from the wagon, "I smell coffee, Adams. What gives?"

"It's not for you, Sawyer."

"What?" Lacy shouted. "Come on, Adams, give us some coffee."

Clint ignored their continued pleas for coffee.

"How much did you make?" Yates asked.

"Enough for us, and that's it."

"I smell beans," Reggie Prince called out.

"It's all gone," Clint called back. "There's no more beans, and no more coffee."

"What about us?" Lacy demanded.

"You'll be fed when you get to Huntsville."

Yates gulped down his beans and coffee and handed the plate and cup back to Clint.

"I have to check on Lincoln," Yates said. "I pushed him hard yesterday."

"I checked on him already," Clint said. "His legs look fine, and there are no stone bruises on his hooves. He came through it in good shape."

"That's good," Yates said. "Thanks."

"All the same, you can drive most of the day. There's no point in making him carry you again so soon."

"Good idea."

"I took the liberty of saddling him," Clint said.

"Why saddle him if I'm not gonna ride him?"

"Just in case," Clint said. "I've decided that if Sawyer's men catch up to us, there's no point in trying to fight them off, not two against thirteen."

"What's the alternative?"

"We'll just mount up and take off, and leave the wagon behind. They won't follow us, they'll go straight to the wagon."

"And free Sawyer."

"Well . . ."

"Well, what?"

"I've made another decision."

"About what?"

"Sawyer," Clint said. "If his men catch up to us, I don't want to leave him behind for them to free."

"But you just said—"

"I said we'd ride off and leave the wagon behind."

Yates frowned.

"Wait a minute . . . you mean you'd kill him?"

"That's what Deputy Fenimore said he'd decided to do, rather than let him go free."

"And did he ask you to do the same?"

"No . . . he didn't ask me. He just told me that was what he'd do."

"Because of his wife."

"Right."

"And what would be your excuse, Clint?"

"I just can't see letting him go free, Gil," Clint said.

"But killing him in cold blood?" Yates asked. "Could you do that?"

"To tell you the truth, I don't know. I guess we'll have to find that out when the time comes."

"Even if you do kill him, they'll track us down."

"I don't think so," Clint said. "How will they know who to track?"

"Do you plan on killing Lacy and Prince, too?"

"No . . ."

"Then they'll tell them."

Clint frowned. He'd thought this over during the night, before Yates had returned, while dozing. obviously, he had not thought it all the way through.

"You're right."

"You'd have to kill all three of them."

"No," Clint said, shaking his head, "even if I could kill Sawyer, I couldn't do it to the other two. They don't deserve that."

Yates looked up at the sky and said, "You'd better think this over some more while we get going."

"You're right," Clint said.

They tied Lincoln to the wagon and then hitched up the team together. Yates climbed aboard the wagon and settled into the seat.

"Did you see my men, Yates?" Sawyer asked.

"I saw them."

"Did you think things over, then? Wanna set me free now?"

"I thought things over, Sawyer, and I came to a decision."

"What decision?"

"If you don't stop chewing my ear off, I'm gonna club you unconscious. If you wake up and start talking again, I'm gonna do it again. If I do it enough times, maybe you won't be around to dance at the end of a rope."

Sawyer was quiet.

"You think about that for a while."

TWENTY-NINE

Clint watched their back trail carefully that day, and found it curious that there wasn't even a hint of a dust cloud. On flat terrain like this such a cloud could be seen for miles, as it had the day before. Why, then, could he not see it now? Could they have gotten that far ahead of the Sawyer Gang? He doubted it.

"What's wrong?" Yates asked him at one point.

"I can't see them," Clint said. "I mean, any sign of them."

Yates halted the wagon, turned around, and looked.

"They can't have gotten further behind," he said. "Did we lose them?"

"Not unless they wanted us to."

"What do you mean?"

"I'm not sure what I mean," Clint said. "Look, they didn't know where we were, right?"

"I guess."

"So they were just riding around, looking for us," Clint said. "What else could they do?"

"I don't know."

"There's one thing that comes to mind."

"What?"

"What if they simply headed for Huntsville?" Clint said. "What if they got to a main road and simply rode on to Huntsville?"

"Then they'd get there ahead of us, because we're not staying to the roads."

"Right."

Yates looked to the front and said, "So they're ahead of us?"

"Could be."

"Waiting for us?"

"It's possible."

Yates frowned.

"What could they do once we reach there?" he asked. "I mean, once we get to the prison it's them who would be outnumbered, not us, right?"

"Right," Clint said, "so they don't wait for us at the prison, they wait between us and the prison."

"They watch the roads, you mean."

"They watch every direction."

"So no matter what direction we come in from, they'll know it?"

"Right."

"So we're beat."

"No."

"Why not?"

"Because in order to watch every direction they have to split up," Clint explained. "That means that we're no longer as outnumbered as we were."

Yates was thinking along with Clint now.

"And when they spot us they won't have time to regroup again."

"We hope."

"That's supposing that we're right about all of this."

"Yes."

Yates turned around again and looked behind them.

"If they were still behind us, we'd see the dust right?"

"We'd have to," Clint said. "There's no way to hide that."

"Okay," Yates said, "so what do we do now?"

"We stop at a town before we get to Huntsville and we send a telegram ahead."

"For help?"

"Right."

"An escort."

"They can either send out an escort, or send out some men to round up Sawyer's gang."

"And if we're right about this," Yates said, "we can get to a main road, where the traveling would be smoother."

"Especially at night."

They sat staring at each other for a while.

"Now what?" Yates asked.

"Well, if we're wrong," Clint said, "getting on a road or stopping in a town could be dangerous."

"Then we have a decision to make," Yates said. "Or you do, since you're in charge."

"Oh, no," Clint said, "we make this decision together. It's your neck, too."

"Well, somebody make a decision," Sawyer said from the wagon. "I can't stand the suspense."

"Let's keep moving," Clint suggested, ignoring Sawyer. "We've got time to make this decision."

Yates nodded and started the team again.

"No decision today?" Sawyer asked.

They both ignored him.

It occurred to Clint over the next half a day's travel that he might be making everything harder than it should be. Maybe they really had lost the gang, maybe they were in the clear. Still, it wouldn't hurt to play it safe and send a telegram ahead to the prison.

THIRTY

They camped that night, and their first decision was whether or not to make a fire.

"This is silly," Clint said finally. "We're paralyzed by indecision."

"It's time to raise or fold," Yates said. "You're a gambler, right?"

"Right. And you?"

"Yep."

"So we raise?" Clint asked.

"We raise."

They made a fire, then set about to making coffee, some beans, and even—while they were raising—some bacon.

"At least if they come in here shooting and wipe us out," Yates said, "we'll both die with a full stomach."

"That's a comfort," Clint said wryly.

"What about them?" Yates asked, nodding toward the prisoners.

"What about them?"

"Do you want to feed them?"

Clint scowled. He didn't relish the thought of giving some of the food to Sawyer. The other two,

122

maybe, but his dislike of Sawyer was growing.

"You can if you want," he said.

Yates looked over at the wagon.

"I'd like to feed the other two and leave Sawyer out," Yates said.

"That would start trouble in the wagon we don't need," Clint said. "Give them each some food."

"Okay."

"And be careful."

"I will."

Yates walked over to the wagon, and both Lacy and Prince pressed their faces to the bars.

"You gonna feed us?" Lacy asked anxiously.

"If you don't try anything, yes," Yates said.

"We won't try nothin', will we, Prince?"

"I'm too hungry to try anythin'," Prince said.

"I'll bring one plate over at a time," Yates said. "You decide who goes first."

Yates went back to the fire and made up one plate of bacon and beans. When he got back to the wagon, Reggie Prince was waiting at the door. Mark Lacy was sitting in a corner, pouting.

"Put one hand out," Yate's said.

"How am I gonna get the plate through the bars?" Prince asked.

Yates saw that the man had a point, and now he was sorry he had offered to feed them. Obviously, he was going to have to open the door.

"I'll get the key," Yates said.

As Yates walked away, Sawyer said, "When that door opens, you fellas be ready."

"Can't we eat first?" Lacy asked.

"This might be our only chance," Sawyer said curtly. "Be ready!"

"Okay," Lacy said, still pouting.

When Yates got back to the fire, Clint asked, "What's the matter?"

"I need the keys," Yates said. "These plates won't fit between the bars."

Clint shook his head.

"Coffee cups."

"What?"

"There are extra coffee cups under the wagon seat," Clint said. "Put the bacon and the beans in the cups. They'll fit between the bars."

Yates frowned.

"Why didn't I think of that?"

"I've done this before, Gil."

"I guess so."

Yates went back to the wagon for the extra cups, then explained to the men what he was doing.

As Yates walked away again, Lacy hissed at Sawyer, "He ain't openin' the door."

"Damn!" Sawyer swore.

"Can we eat now?" Lacy asked.

"Reggie," Sawyer said.

"Yeah?"

"If you get a chance, you grab that boy, you hear? You hold him so we can get his gun."

"I'll hold him," Prince said, in spite of the fact

that his stomach was growling.

"After we get his gun and we make Adams let us out," Sawyer went on, "then we can eat."

"All right!" Lacy said.

"And then you can snap the boy's neck, Reggie," Sawyer added.

"Like a twig, Sawyer," the big black man said, "like a twig."

THIRTY-ONE

As Yates returned to the wagon he saw that Lacy was now the man waiting at the door. Why they had changed their minds he didn't know, but he didn't think much of it.

That was his mistake.

He walked up to the wagon and said, "Put one arm out between the bars, Lacy."

"Sure, Cap'n," Lacy said.

He stuck his hand out, and Yates reached out and handed him one of the cups he was holding.

"Don't sneeze, Lacy," Sawyer said, "or the brave man will drop your food."

Lacy brought his food into the wagon then skittered into a corner to eat it with the spoon Yates had provided. Clint had warned him not to give them any forks.

"Spoons are bad enough," Clint said, "but they won't have them long enough to turn them into weapons. Besides, they're pretty hungry."

"Who's next?" Yates asked.

"Me, friend," Sawyer said, moving to the door. "Put your arm out."

"Yessir!"

Sawyer stuck his arm out, and Yates carefully placed the cup in the man's hand. Sawyer was the one he expected to try something, and when the man simply took his food and moved to the back of the wagon, Yates was surprised.

"Me last, Cap'n," Prince said.

"Put your arm out," Yates said, holding out a cup.

Prince tried, but apparently his arm was thicker than Sawyer's and Lacy's.

"You got to come closer, mister," Prince said. "I can't reach."

Yates hesitated, then with one hand on his gun he moved closer, holding the cup out. He was still puzzling over Sawyer's failure to try something, and so was surprised when Reggie Prince's other arm came shooting out through the bars and grabbed him by the shirtfront.

"Clint!" he shouted.

Prince pulled him against the door hard, and his forehead struck the bars, stunning him. The cup of food went flying from one hand as his other hand tightened on the gun.

"Turn him around!" he heard Sawyer shout.

Jesus, Yates thought, his air suddenly cut off, *I'm gonna die!*

Should have stayed behind the bar!

Clint heard Yates's strangled cry and leapt to his feet. By the time Clint got to the wagon, Yates was pinned against it with one of Reggie Prince's massive arms around his throat.

"Get his gun!" he heard Sawyer shout.

"Don't try it!" Clint warned.

Before anyone could do anything, Yates drew his gun and tossed it away into the darkness. He was almost unconscious, and it was a last-ditch effort on his part to do something useful in the situation.

"Let him loose, Prince," Clint said, gun in hand.

"Where's his gun?" Sawyer shouted.

"He threw it away," Prince said.

"Damn!" Sawyer swore. Then he said, "This can still work, Prince. Hold him still."

"I got him," Prince said. "He ain't goin' now-heres."

"Adams, unlock the door or I'll have Reggie here snap the kid's neck."

"I don't think so, Sawyer."

"Don't think I won't," Prince said.

"Clint . . ." Yates rasped, "don't . . ."

"Shut up!" Prince said, and squeezed tighter. Yates's eyes were almost bulging right out of their sockets.

"Let him go, Reggie," Clint said.

"Don't let him go, Reggie," Sawyer said.

"I ain't."

"We got a standoff, Adams," Sawyer said. "Unlock the door or the kid dies."

"I don't think so, Sawyer," Clint said again.

"Why ain't he openin' the door?" Reggie Prince demanded, wide-eyed.

"Reggie," Clint said, "I'll bet your arm is so thick that I could put a bullet in it without it going through."

"Huh? What's he talkin' about?" Prince asked Sawyer.

"Don't listen to him, Reggie," Sawyer said. "He's tryin' to scare you."

"No, I'm not," Clint said. "Look at Reggie's arm, Sawyer. The bullet will never go through and hit Yates, believe me."

"Kill 'im, Reggie," Sawyer said. "Snap his neck."

"Yeah, go ahead, Reggie," Clint said. He could feel the sweat running down his back beneath his shirt. "Kill him, and I kill you. You're heading for Huntsville for what, five years? How would you like to be dead, instead?"

"Don't listen to him, Reggie," Sawyer said, "listen to me."

"Yeah, listen to Sawyer, Reggie," Clint said. "What does he care if you die? He's heading for a rope anyway."

"Reggie!" Sawyer shouted. "Damn it, kill him!"

"If you kill him, Reggie," Clint said, "I'll kill you, and then I'll take Lacy and Sawyer into Huntsville. You're the only one of the three who'll be dead."

"Reggie!"

"Shut up, Sawyer!" Prince snapped. The sweat was running down from his forehead into his eyes, stinging. "Let me think!"

"No time to think, Reggie," Clint said. He

thumbed back the hammer on his gun and added, "Let him go . . . now!"

"Kill him!" Sawyer shouted.

"Damn!" Prince screamed and released Yates, who slumped to the ground. "I ain't dyin' for you, Sawyer."

"Jesus," Sawyer snapped, "you stupid black bastard!"

Prince turned on Sawyer, his eyes blazing, and advanced on him. Sawyer shrank back and said, "Now, wait a minute, Reggie."

Prince's hand snapped out and took hold of Sawyer by the throat.

"You don't talk to me no more, you hear?" he said. "No more, from here to Huntsville. If'n you do, I'll snap your neck and save the hangman the bother. You understand?"

"Yeah, sure, Reggie," Sawyer said, nodding as best he could with the big man's hand around his throat, "I understand."

Prince released Sawyer, then turned back around and asked Clint, "I get some food?"

"Sure, Reggie," Clint said, helping Yates to his feet, "I'll get you some food."

"Thanks, Mister," Prince said. Then to Yates he said, "Hey, no hard feelin's, friend."

"Jesus," Yates rasped, rubbing his neck, "he almost kills me and now he wants to be friends."

THIRTY-TWO

Clint and Yates sat by the fire. They had retrieved Yates's gun from the darkness and it was back in his holster where it belonged. Every so often Yates would reach up and touch his throat.

"I'm sorry," he said, apologizing for the umpteenth time.

"I told you," Clint said, "you've got nothing to be sorry about."

"They fooled me," Yates said. "When the first two didn't try anything—especially Sawyer—I didn't expect Prince—"

"Gil, look," Clint said, "forget it. You're the one who suffered for it, so stop apologizing."

"You saved my life."

"Maybe I did—"

"You know, I thought about not coming back," Yates confessed.

"I figured you might," Clint said, "but you did come back, didn't you?"

"Yeah, I did."

"That's what matters, then," Clint said. "Why

131

don't you get some sleep and I'll take the first watch."

"Why did you feed Prince?" Yates asked. He blurted it out, as if it was something that had been bothering him.

"He was hungry."

"Yeah, but he tried to escape," Yates said, "he tried to kill me."

"If he'd wanted to kill you, you'd be dead, Gil," Clint said. "He was pushed into it by Sawyer. He's the one you should be mad at, not Prince."

"If you don't mind," Yates said, "I think I'll stay mad at all three of them. They can starve from here on out, for all I care."

"That's up to you," Clint said. "Go ahead, turn in. You need some rest."

Yates touched his neck and said, "I'd just as soon take the first watch. I'd kind of like to sit and think for a while."

"Don't torture yourself over it, Gil."

"I'd like to just sit here and be glad I'm alive, okay?" Yates said. "I really thought I was going to die."

"Okay," Clint said, "whichever way you want to play it."

The younger man had learned a hard lesson, the kind men usually paid for with their lives. It would do him some good to sit and think it over, so Clint decided to go ahead and give him the time to do it.

Not too much time, though. Once the lesson was learned, a man had to go on from there. File it in the back of his mind and forget it.

Clint hoped that Yates would be able to do that, and that this wouldn't drive him back to tending bar.

He rolled himself up in his blanket and went to sleep.

Jeff Sawyer sat in a corner of the prison wagon, watching Reggie Prince clean out his cup of beans and bacon. He wanted to say something to Prince, tell him what a fool he'd been, and that they were all still prisoners because of him. If he did that, however, he was sure that the black man would kill him. Tonight was not the night to say anything more to the man.

Sawyer figured he had one more night after this one before they reached Huntsville. His men had that long to free him. He knew Billy July wanted to take over the gang for himself, but he didn't think that would stop July from trying to free him. There were enough men in the gang who were loyal to Sawyer who wouldn't let July just forget it. Besides, July could never really earn the respect needed to control the gang unless he took control from Sawyer. Taking over only because Sawyer was in jail wouldn't prove July's superiority.

July was going to have to free him just so they could struggle for control of the gang. After all, that's what he'd do.

THIRTY-THREE

Not everyone agreed with Billy July's decision to abandon the search for the prison wagon.

"Jeff's countin' on us to get him out," Zeke Styles said. "He's gonna be waitin' for us."

"And we're going to be waiting for him," July said, "right outside of Huntsville."

"It's too dangerous," Styles said. "It's too close to the prison."

July ignored Styles and spoke to the rest of the men.

"We can go traipsing all over Texas, and if we don't find them Sawyer will end up in Huntsville. One way or another, they'll show up there. It makes more sense to go there and wait."

"If they're not there already," one of the other men, Powell, said.

"I don't think so," July said. "After that run-in we had with them, I don't think they'll make Huntsville until day after tomorrow. Not at the pace they'll have to keep with that wagon. Plus, they know we're looking for them, so they'll stay off the main roads. We have a chance to beat them to Huntsville, and then we'll be waiting for them."

"I still don't know," Styles said, shaking his head.

July saw some of the other men frowning or shaking their heads as well.

"Okay, look," he said, "Turner, Kendall, Blevins, and me, we're heading for Huntsville. The rest of you can do what you want."

"We're with you, Billy," a man named Tatum said. "Right?"

He looked around, and most of the men began to nod their heads.

"What about you, Powell?" July asked.

Powell looked around and realized he was now outnumbered.

"Yeah, sure, Billy," he said, "I'm with you."

"Styles?"

"Hell, if everybody's goin', I'm goin', too," Styles said.

"Good," July said. "We'll break camp early in the morning and head straight for Huntsville."

They had two camp fires going, and while July and Turner sat at one, the rest of the men milled about the other one.

"For a while there I didn't think they'd go along," Turner said.

"They'll always go along," July said. "You just have to force them to make a choice."

"What do you think is gonna happen, Billy?" Turner asked.

"Me?" July asked. "I think Sawyer's gonna hang, Tally."

"Is that what you want?"

"He's a killer," July said. "You saw what he did to that deputy's woman."

"But the others—"

"The others followed him, Tally," July said, "except you, me, and a couple of others. Once he raped her, the others did it also, but he was the one who killed her. It's murder that brings the attention to you, don't you know that? We'll be a lot better off pulling jobs without him and not killing anybody."

Turner had to agree that he'd seen Sawyer kill for no reason more times than once.

"You're no murderer, Tally."

"No, I ain't."

"There's no money in killing, only attention— the kind we don't need. You'll see. When I take over, you'll see how things change."

"I hope you're right," Turner said.

"Sure I'm right," July said. "Have we made any money in the past couple of weeks?"

"No," Turner said, "but we was waitin' for Sawyer to be sentenced, and then we started tryin' to find that prison wagon."

"All because he killed some people without cause," July said. "Do you see what I mean? We could have pulled off one big bank job instead of all this, and we'd all be rolling in money."

The longer July talked, the more Turner nodded his head in agreement.

"I'll need you to back me, Tally," July said. "When you do that, some of the others will follow—like Kendall and Blevins—and then the rest."

Turner thought it over.

"Can I count on you, Tally?"

Turner thought some more and then said, "Yeah, sure, Billy. You can count on me."

"Good," July said. He pulled a bottle of whiskey from his saddlebag. "Let's have a drink on it."

He poured some whiskey into his coffee and then some into Turner's.

At the other fire Powell, Styles, and a couple of the other men were talking, while the rest turned in.

"We got to watch July," Styles said. "He wants Sawyer to hang so he can take over."

"If that's the case," a man named Forrester asked, "why is he going through all this?"

"So it looks good, that's why," Styles said.

"You sayin' he wants Sawyer to hang?" Powell asked.

"That's what I'm sayin'."

"Well, we ain't gonna let that happen, are we?" a man called Del Curry asked.

"No," Styles said, "we ain't. You fellas just watch me and wait for my signal."

"To do what?" Powell asked.

Styles looked at Powell and said, "Whatever it takes to free Sawyer, that's what."

THIRTY-FOUR

Over coffee the next morning Clint asked Yates how his neck felt.

"Sore," Yates said, touching his throat and wincing. "That Prince has an arm like an iron bar." He looked over at the wagon and added, "With any luck Prince killed Sawyer during the night."

"I don't think so," Clint said, "but we can check."

Clint walked over to the wagon and looked inside. He saw Sawyer staring back at him.

"Still alive?" Clint asked. "Guess you didn't try talking to Reggie during the night, did you?"

No answer.

"No smart remarks this morning, Sawyer?" he asked. "No warnings? No offers of big money?"

Sawyer sneered.

"I'm through offerin' you a chance to live, Adams," he said. "You and that kid are dead, as far as I'm concerned, and I don't talk to dead men."

"That's fine with us, Sawyer," Clint said. "That's just fine with us."

• • •

They saddled their horses and hitched up the team and got moving early. There were still no remarks from Sawyer, and since he wasn't talking, neither were the other two. For the first time since they'd started their trek they were riding in silence.

They took the wagon to the nearest road and started traveling along it. Before long they came to a town called Perry, and Clint was glad to see telegraph wires strung in the vicinity.

"We'll stop and see the sheriff first," Clint said, "and get the prisoners placed in his cells."

"And then a good meal?" Yates asked.

"And then a good meal," Clint agreed.

They drove the prison wagon right down the main street, attracting a lot of attention, and stopped in front of the sheriff's office.

"Stay here with them," Clint said, dismounting. "I'll go in and talk to the sheriff."

"Right."

As Clint entered the sheriff's office, a crowd of people began to gather around the wagon, trying to see inside.

"Mister?" a small boy called up to Yates.

He looked around and then down, locating the source of the voice. It was a small, towheaded boy of about eight.

"Yes?"

"You got any killers in there?" the boy asked, pointing.

"Where's your mother?" Yates asked.

• • •

"Sheriff?"

The man behind the desk looked up and smiled. He looked more like a storekeeper than a sheriff. As the lawman stood up, Clint thought he would have looked more comfortable with an apron around his substantial midsection than the gun belt he was wearing.

"I'm Sheriff Walters."

"My name's Clint Adams, Sheriff."

"What can I do for you, Mr. Adams?" the man asked, showing no hint of recognition.

"I've got a prison wagon outside, Sheriff. I'm transporting three prisoners to Huntsville. I'd like to store them in your jail while I send a telegraph ahead."

"Are you a lawman, Mr. Adams?"

"No, I'm not."

"You work for the prison, then?"

"Uh, no, sir, I don't."

The man frowned.

"Would you mind telling me how you came to be transporting three prisoners to Huntsville Prison, then?" Sheriff Walters asked.

"It's a long story, Sheriff," Clint said. "Could we get them inside before I tell it?"

"I don't think so, Mr. Adams," Walters said, folding his arms across his chest. "I think I'd like to hear the story before I offer you my facilities."

Well, Clint thought, maybe the man was a real lawman after all.

"Well, all right," Clint said. "It started . . ."

· · ·

After Clint told the lawman his story, he waited for the man to say something.

"Would you have any proof of this?" the sheriff asked.

"What kind of proof?"

"A letter, perhaps, from this deputy marshal you mentioned?"

"No," Clint said, "I don't have a letter, but I've got better proof than that."

"What kind of proof?"

"I've got a wagon outside with three prisoners in it, Sheriff," Clint said. "What more proof do you need?"

THIRTY-FIVE

Sheriff Walters agreed to put the prisoners in his cells, but he told Clint he was going to check up on his story.

When the wagon was empty they drove it over to the livery, where they paid in advance to have it housed and to have the two team horses and their own looked after.

"You might want to look the wagon over, also," Clint said. "We drove it over some pretty rough ground."

"I'll do 'er," the liveryman said.

They left the livery with their saddlebags and rifles and headed for a saloon they had passed on the way down the main street.

"A beer first," Clint said, "then the telegraph office."

"Then a hot meal?" Yates asked.

"Actually," Clint said, "there's no reason you have to come over to the telegraph office with me. You can start eating while I do that, and then I'll join you."

"I won't argue with that."

They went to the saloon and each had a beer, all the while suffering the curious stares of the other patrons. Apparently, someone recognized them as having brought the wagon into town, and the word got around.

"Thanks," Clint said, paying the bartender for the two beers.

"Another round?" the man asked.

"I don't think so," Clint said. "I've got holes in my back from prying eyes."

"They're just curious, is all," the bartender said. "Like to know who you brung into town in that wagon."

"Maybe if they asked," Clint said, "I'd tell them."

He and Yates turned around and walked out of the saloon.

"There's a little café across the street," Clint pointed out. "That seems as good a place as any to eat. Here, take my saddlebags, too, and I'll join you after I've sent the telegram."

"Okay."

Yates walked across to the café while Clint went in search of the telegraph office. He had to ask directions to find it. Once he did find it and had pencil in hand to write his message, he realized he was stumped. How was he going to explain all of this in a few words?

"Is there a problem?" the clerk asked.

"I'm thinking," Clint said.

"Is that what you were doin'?" the man asked. "Don't get much of that around here."

Clint ignored the man and started writing, trying to keep it as succinct as possible. What he finally ended up with was this: FENIMORE INJURED IN CULPEPPER, TEXAS. HAVE TAKEN OVER ASSIGNMENT. NEED HELP.

He signed it: CLINT ADAMS, PERRY, TEXAS.

"Okay," Clint said, handing the flimsy over to the clerk, "send it."

"You gonna wait for a reply?"

Clint hesitated, then said, "No, I'll be at that café across from the saloon."

"You want me to bring the answer over there?" the man asked, looking aghast at the prospect.

"Is that a problem?"

"I got nobody to watch this place," the man said. "Somethin' of great value might get stole."

"I'll come back and check in with you after I've eaten," Clint said. "I sure wouldn't want something of great value to get stole on account of me."

"Me, neither," the man said, and sat down at his key. He was clattering away on it as Clint left.

When Clint got to the café there was a pot of coffee and two cups on the table in front of Yates.

"You're a lifesaver," Clint said. He sat and poured himself a full cup.

"I ordered for you, too," Yates said. "Steak and vegetables. I hope that was all right."

"That's fine," Clint said.

"Did you get the message sent?"

"Yes," Clint said. "We'll check back there after we eat to see if we got an answer."

Their lunch was brought over by a man who looked like the sheriff, only with an apron instead of a gun belt.

Halfway through the meal the liveryman appeared at the door and then moved to their table.

"Thought you might be here," he said. "Heard you talkin' 'bout gettin' somethin' to eat."

"What brings you here?" Clint asked. "Something wrong with one of the horses?"

"No," the man said, "but you got a busted rear axle on that wagon."

"What?" Yates said.

"How could we have gotten this far with a busted axle?" Clint asked.

"I'd guess you didn't. It's cracked, and it probably cracked just a short time ago."

"Can we ride on it?"

"You can."

"Good."

"But it's gonna bust clean through first good bump you hit."

"Shit," Yates said.

"Can you fix it?" Clint asked.

"Could."

"Good."

"If I had a replacement."

"And do you?"

"Nope."

"Can you get one?"

"Could."

"But?"

"Take four, five days, maybe a week."

"We can't stay here that long," Yates said.

"We may not have to," Clint said.

"What do you mean?" Yates asked.

Clint held up a hand for Yates to wait and told the liveryman, "Go ahead and do what you've got to do."

"New axle's gonna cost."

"You'll be paid," Clint said, "by the state of Texas."

"Well, that's right nice," the man said, "but I'm gonna need a deposit before I send for that axle."

Clint frowned, then took out some money and dickered with the man until they agreed on the deposit.

"Don't see what you're dickerin' for," the liveryman said, before leaving. "If I'm gettin' paid by the state of Texas, you'll get your deposit back, too, won't ya?"

"Could," Clint said.

"Huh?"

"Never mind," Clint said. "We'd like to finish our lunch."

"Sure, go ahead," the man said. "I'll start lookin' for somebody that's got an axle."

"You do that."

After the man left, Yates leaned forward and said, "We gonna sit here for a week waiting for an axle?"

"No," Clint said. "Once I get an answer to my telegraph message I'll send another one describing our situation and they'll send someone to replace us."

"Well, I'm glad to hear that," Yates said, attacking his plate again. "Be a pleasure to be rid of Sawyer and those other two."

"I know what you mean."

Yates chewed a piece of meat thoughtfully, then asked, "Are you sure about that?"

"About what?"

"That they'll send replacements?"

"Well . . . almost sure," Clint said. "Besides, you won't have to wait around. I'll do that. You can be on your way."

"On my way . . ."

"Right."

Yates frowned. "That's funny."

"What is?"

"I can't think where I'll go."

"Well," Clint said, "there's no hurry to decide, is there?"

"No," Yates said, "I guess not."

THIRTY-SIX

They walked back to the telegraph office together, and Yates waited outside while Clint went in to see if a reply had come back.

Clint came out almost immediately and said, "No reply yet."

"What do we do now?" Yates asked, handing Clint back his saddlebags.

"Get a hotel room, I guess," Clint said, "if we're going to be stuck here awhile."

"Well," Yates said, "at least we get to sleep on real beds tonight."

Clint nodded and they started walking toward the hotel.

"Sawyer's gang is going to be surprised when we don't show up."

"Let them."

"Sawyer, Lacy, and Prince, too."

"So they get an extra day or two before they go into the prison."

When they reached the hotel and entered the lobby, Yates said, "One room or two?"

"Two, I think," Clint said. "I like having my

own room. Is that a problem?"

"Uh . . ."

"I'll pay for both."

"Why should you do that?"

"Because you don't have any money."

"Well, there is that," Yates admitted.

"And I'll probably get it back later."

"I hope so."

They walked up to the desk clerk and asked for two rooms.

"You're lucky we ain't busy," the clerk said. He was a short, bespectacled man with a walrus mustache that completely covered his mouth.

"You have two rooms, then?"

"Hell," the man said, "we got ten. Take your pick."

"Something without a balcony or ledge on the outside," Clint said.

"That'd be room four," the man said.

"I'll just take the room closest to that one," Yates said.

"That'd be five. Sign the book, please."

They each signed the book in turn and accepted their keys. The clerk turned the book around and read both names out loud.

"Gil Yates and . . . *Clint Adams*?"

"That's right," Clint said.

The clerk's eyes got watery behind his glasses as he stared at Clint.

"Welcome to our hotel, uh, gents. Anything w-we can do for you, don't h-hesitate to ask."

"Thanks," Clint said. "We'll do that."

On the way up the stairs Yates asked, "What'd he get so nervous about?"

"It happens sometimes."

"Why—oh, you mean he recognized your name?"

"I guess."

Yates seemed impressed with that.

They walked to their rooms and Clint said, "I'm going to get a bath. If I'm going to be here awhile I might as well get the trail off me."

"Sounds good to me," Yates said. "Besides, you never know when you'll run into a young lady."

"I hope they've got facilities right here in the hotel," Clint said. "I'll meet you downstairs in ten minutes, okay?"

"Fine."

They both went into their rooms to get clean clothes from their saddlebags and to be alone with their thoughts.

THIRTY-SEVEN

Clint was getting ready to leave his room when there was a knock on the door. He figured it was Yates and was surprised to find the sheriff standing outside his room.

"I think you're waiting for this," the man said, handing him a telegram.

Clint frowned and asked, "Why are you delivering my telegram?"

"Because I was trying to send one of my own," Walters said. "Can I come in?"

"Is there something I can do for you?" Clint asked. "I was on my way to take a bath."

"You could let me in so I can talk to you," the sheriff said. "I won't keep you long."

"Okay," Clint said, "come on in."

The sheriff entered, and Clint closed the door and turned to face him.

"Don't you want to read your telegram?"

Clint looked down at the piece of paper in his hand, then back at the lawman.

"Why do I have the feeling you've already read it?" he asked.

"I have."

"Well, then, why don't you tell me what it says?"

"It's from the prison authorities in Huntsville," Walters said. "Apparently, they want you to prove who you are before they'll send assistance out to you."

"Uh-huh," Clint said. "That's what you want, too, right? For me to prove my claim?"

"Well," Walters said, "it would be helpful. See, I tried to send a telegram to that town you told me about, Culpepper?"

"They don't have a telegraph office."

"I found that out," Walters said. "So how can I verify your story?"

"I do have three prisoners, don't I?"

"Yes, you do."

"And a prison wagon."

"You have that, too," Walters said. "The question is, do you have the authority to be in possession of the wagon and the prisoners."

"I don't have any way of proving that, Sheriff."

Walters frowned.

"Did you ask the prisoners?"

"Yes, I did," the sheriff said. "They claim they're innocent."

"Huntsville is full of innocent men, isn't it, Sheriff?"

"I guess so."

"So," Clint asked, "what do we do now?"

Walters rubbed his jaw thoughtfully.

"Well, I'm willing to keep the prisoners in my jail until you can prove your claim."

"For how long?"

"Oh, until tomorrow."

"And then what?"

"Well, I guess I'll have to set them free."

"I tell you what, Sheriff," Clint said. "While I'm busy trying to prove my claim, why don't you go back to your office and look through your wanted posters? When you find the one on Jeff Sawyer, compare it to the man you have in your cell. Would you do that?"

"That sounds like a good idea."

"Good," Clint said. "Meanwhile, I'll see what I can do about proving everything I've told you."

The sheriff turned to leave, then turned back.

"I know who you are, Mr. Adams."

"You do?"

"Of course," he said. "It's my job to know people like you."

"I see."

"Don't think you can intimidate me."

"Sheriff?"

"Yes?"

"What did you do just before you got this job?"

"Why . . . I was a schoolteacher."

"Why doesn't that surprise me?"

"Excuse me?"

"Never mind, Sheriff," Clint said, patting the man on the shoulder. "I'll talk to you later."

Clint ushered the man out of the room and then tried to decide if he had the time to spend on a bath.

Well, maybe later.

THIRTY-EIGHT

Clint left the hotel without saying anything to Gil Yates, who he assumed was already in a bathtub. There was no sense in making the man get out.

He went to the telegraph office and sent off another telegraph message to Huntsville, this one with a little more detail. He couldn't prove that he was authorized to transport the prisoners, but there could certainly be no doubt that he had them.

When he received a telegram back, it asked for exactly that, proof that he actually had these prisoners. That meant he had to get the sheriff to send a message to Huntsville backing up his claim.

He left the telegraph office and walked to the sheriff's office.

"I can't do that, Adams."

"Why not?" Clint asked. "All you have to do is look in your cells to see that I have them."

"I see three men," Walters said. "I don't know who those men are."

"This is insane," Clint said. "I've got three men who are supposed to be in prison, and I can't get them there."

"Why not just take them yourself?"

"I've got a broken axle on the wagon, Sheriff," Clint said. "I might not be able to leave here for a week."

"Well," Walters said, "before I'll send a telegram saying I have Jeff Sawyer in my jail, you'll have to prove that to me."

Clint stared at the sheriff, then looked at the ceiling and said, "This is making me dizzy."

He turned and walked out without another word to the sheriff.

"I was wondering where you got off to," Yates said as he let Clint into his room.

"Come on," Clint said, "I need a drink."

"What's been happening?"

"I'll tell you over at the saloon."

Once they were seated at a table with their beers, Clint told Yates about his conversations with the sheriff.

"Boy," Yates said, "I'll bet you didn't expect this when you agreed to do this favor."

"I don't know what I expected," Clint said wearily. "I don't know why I do these things."

"What things?"

"Get myself involved in other people's business," Clint said.

"You do it a lot?"

"It's a bad habit of mine I can't seem to shake."

"Well, what do we do now?"

"I don't know," Clint said. "I've got to think about it."

"First a broken axle, and now we can't get anyone to believe us," Yates said. "What else could go wrong?"

At that moment thirteen men rode into Perry from the south end of town.

"First the livery stable," Billy July said, "then the saloon."

"We gettin' hotel rooms?" Powell asked.

"No," July said, "we are not staying. We'll get some supplies after we hit the saloon and keep on going."

They rode to the livery, where they raised the eyebrows of the liveryman.

"Don't know if I got room for all these horses," he said.

"You can just put them in a corral," July said. "You got a corral, don't you?"

"You don't wanna put them up for the night?"

"Just for a few hours," July said.

"Corral's out back," the man said. "You can take 'em there."

"Let's go," July said.

The thirteen men rode their horses around to the back and toward the corral, and they all stopped short when they saw the wagon out behind the livery.

"Billy?" Tally Turner said.

"I see it," July said. "Kendall?"

"Yeah, Billy?"

"Go and get that liveryman out here."

"Sure, Billy."

The big man dismounted and walked into the livery through the back door. He had to circle around the prison wagon to do it, and he did so without looking at it. He wouldn't want anybody to know, but the thing scared him.

"What do we do now, Billy?" Turner asked.

"First," July said, "we get these horses taken care of, and then we'll talk to the liveryman." He turned to look at the others and, even though he personally didn't feel that it was true, said, "Boys, it looks like we walked into a piece of luck."

THIRTY-NINE

Clint and Yates were each working on a second beer, trying to come up with a solution to their problem.

"There's only one thing I can think of," Clint finally said.

"What's that?"

"The sheriff must have a poster on Sawyer."

"Did you ask him?"

"I suggested he look for one," Clint said, "but I think maybe we should go over and help him look."

"If he doesn't have one, what do we do then?" Yates asked.

Clint hesitated, then said, "Well, maybe we should just leave Sawyer and the others where they are and leave town. Let Walters worry about it. After all, he's a lawman and we're not."

"He already said he'd cut them loose, didn't he?"

"Yeah," Clint said, "he said it, but I don't know if he'd do it. My guess is he'd have somebody federal come in and take a look at the three of them before he set them free."

As they stood up, Yates said, "You mean you hope he'd do that. It'd be a shame if Sawyer was let go because of a cracked axle, wouldn't it?"

"Yeah," Clint said, "it would."

As they left the saloon, he wondered how he'd ever be able to explain that to Tom Fenimore.

Kendall came out of the stable with the liveryman in tow. The man had a horrified look on his face.

"I didn't do nothin', mister," he was saying to the big man.

"Shut up," Kendall said. "Here he is, Billy."

"What's he draggin' me out here for, mister?" the liveryman asked July. "I ain't done nothin'."

"Just answer a few questions, friend," July said, "and you won't have any problems. When did that wagon come into town?"

The man turned and stared at the wagon, then looked back at July.

"The prison wagon?"

"That's right."

"It came in earlier today," he said. "It's got a cracked axle."

"How many men driving it?"

"One drivin'," the man said, "and one ridin' alongside."

"Two men?" July asked. "That's all?"

"That's it."

"How many men inside?"

"Three."

"Where are they now?"

"In the jail, I heard."

"And the two men?"

"I dunno," he said. "Maybe the hotel, maybe the saloon."

"You happen to know who the two men were?"

"One I do, one I don't."

"Who's the man you do know?"

"Clint Adams."

"Billy," Turner said, "that's—"

"I know who he is, Tally," July said, cutting him off. He looked back at the liveryman and asked, "Was Adams wearing a badge?"

"Not that I saw."

"The other man?"

"I don't think so."

July looked away and said, more to himself than aloud,

"No badges."

"Mister," the liveryman said, "can I go now?"

July looked at the man. He knew that if Jeff Sawyer was there he'd kill the man to keep him quiet. Actually, in this case it sounded like a pretty good idea. If they let the man go, he was sure to run to the local sheriff.

As if reading his mind, the liveryman said, "Listen, mister, I won't tell nobody you're here, or that you was asking about the wagon. Honest."

"You won't, huh?"

"No, I swear."

"The fact that you brought it up means that you were thinking about it, doesn't it?"

"Huh? I wasn't thinkin' about nothing. I don't do much thinkin', ask anybody in town."

"I don't have the time to ask anybody, friend," July said. He looked at Kendall and nodded.

"Huh?" Kendall asked.

"Take care of him, Kendall."

"What do you want me to do with him, Billy?" Kendall asked, confused.

Tally Turner went over to Kendall and whispered in his ear.

"Oh!" Kendall said. "Okay. Come on." He pulled the liveryman back into the stable, this time literally dragging him as the man tried to resist. His boot heels left two deep grooves all the way to the stable door.

"What do we do now, Billy?" Turner asked.

"We locate Adams and this other man," July said. "We've got to identify them before we can make a move. Also, we've got to locate the jail."

"Let's go, then," Turner said.

"Take it easy," July said. "We can't all go walking through town. We'll attract too much attention. Anybody here know what Clint Adams looks like?"

No answer.

"Nobody's ever seen him?"

"I seen a drawing once," Blevins said.

"A drawing?" July asked. "Where'd you see a drawing?"

Blevins looked embarrassed.

"In one of them dime novels," he admitted.

A few men started to laugh, including Turner.

"You read one of them things?"

"Yeah," Blevins said. "I had nothin' better to do at the time."

More laughter, and then July called a halt to it.

"Never mind," he said, waving his hand. "Tally, you and Blevins take a walk around town and see if you can spot Adams and this other man."

"Okay, Billy."

"Powell?"

"Yeah?"

"You and me are going to see if we can find the sheriff's office."

"Right."

"What about the rest of us?" Styles asked.

"The rest of you just stay here and wait," July said. "We'll be back soon. By then I'll know what we're gonna do next."

"What we're gonna do next," Styles muttered as July and the others walked away, "is break Sawyer out and get our real leader back."

FORTY

Turner and Blevins were walking down the street when they saw two men crossing over from the other side.

"Hold it," Blevins said.

"What?"

Blevins narrowed his eyes and stared.

"What is it, Blevins?"

"That's him."

"Which one?"

"The older one, of course," Blevins said.

Now it was Turner's turn to squint.

"Are you sure?"

"No, I ain't," Blevins said, "but it sure looks like the drawing I saw."

"Cross," Turner said.

"Wha—"

"Cross the street," Turner said, pushing Blevins. "I want to see where they're goin', and I don't want them to see us."

The two men crossed over as casually as they could, although they each felt like running. Once they got to the other side, they moved to a door-

way and looked across at Clint Adams and Gil
Yates just as the two men went through a door.

"What is that place?" Turner asked. "Where'd
they go in?"

"Jesus," Blevins said.

"What?"

Blevins looked at him and said, "They went
into the sheriff's office."

"We got to find Billy," Turner said.

As Clint and Yates entered, the sheriff looked
up from his desk. As they approached, Clint could
see that the man was going through posters.

"Find him yet, Sheriff?" Clint asked.

"No, not yet," Walters said.

"This is Gil Yates, Sheriff," Clint said. "I don't
think I introduced you fellas before."

"Howdy," the sheriff said.

"You mind if I go in the back and talk to the
prisoners, Sheriff?" Clint asked.

"Go ahead."

"Gil," Clint said, "why don't you help the sheriff find that poster."

"Sure, Clint."

Clint left the two of them leafing though paper
and went in the back where Sawyer, Prince, and
Lacy were occupying individual cells. The cells
were made up of grids, instead of the usual ver-
tical bars.

Lacy came to the front of his cell and put his
face in one of the squares.

"When do we get fed?"

"Shut up," Clint said.

"A little upset, are we, Adams?" Sawyer taunted. His previous bravado seemed to have returned. "The sheriff told us you were havin' a little trouble provin' your story. We tried to help by answerin' all his questions, but our answers only seemed to confuse him more."

"I'll bet," Clint said. "You told him how innocent you were."

"Well, sure," Sawyer said.

"You're only postponing your trip to the gallows, Sawyer."

"Well," Sawyer said, "wouldn't you?"

The man had a point there.

"Send the sheriff back here again, Adams, and we'll try to help him some more," Sawyer said, smiling.

Clint looked at Lacy, who again asked, "When do we get fed?"

In the third cell Reggie Prince was lying on his back, staring at the ceiling. The incident from the previous night seemed to have taken his energy away.

"Don't get too comfortable, Sawyer," Clint said. "I'll have you out of here in no time."

"I doubt it."

Clint turned and went back into the office.

Turner and Blevins saw July and Powell walking toward them and waved them down.

"You don't have to go looking for the jail," Turner said.

"Why not?"

"We found it," Blevins said.

"And Adams is inside."

"Are you sure?" July asked, looking at Blevins. Blevins licked his lips, then nodded shortly and said, "I'm sure. It's him."

"And he's in the jail?"

"Yep," Turner said, "and Sawyer's probably in there, too."

July frowned.

"What if he's not?"

"Where else would they keep him, Billy?" Turner asked. "We got to move now that we got them in one place."

"What if the sheriff's not inside?"

"What if he is?" Turner asked. "We can't afford to wait, Billy."

July thought some more, but he couldn't see any way out of it. Ah hell, maybe Sawyer would catch a bullet.

"Okay," he said, turning to Powell. "Go and get the rest of the men . . . and hurry!"

FORTY-ONE

"Well, I'll be . . ." Clint heard the sheriff say as he came back into the office.

"Find it?"

"Yeah, I did," Walters said, holding out the poster.

Clint took it and looked at it. The drawing was a pretty damned good likeness of Jeff Sawyer.

"Well, Sheriff," he said, "you can retire this one. As you can see, you've already got him in your cell."

"No," Walters said, "*you've* got him in my cell, Mr. Adams."

Clint handed the poster back.

"I appreciate you not saying I told you so," the sheriff said to Clint.

"Sheriff," Clint said, "I'd appreciate it if you'd send a telegram to the authorities at Huntsville Prison."

"Of course," Sheriff Walters said. "I'll do it right now."

"I'll walk over with you," Clint said. "Gil, why don't you stay here with the prisoners."

"Okay."

The sheriff headed for the door, with Clint behind him. As the man opened the door there was a shot. Clint heard hot lead hit flesh, and the sheriff was jolted back into his arms.

Clint staggered under the sheriff's weight, trying to lower him to the ground, as he shouted to Yates, "Close the door!"

Yates went for the door low and slammed it closed, then turned to look at Clint and Walters.

Clint took one look at the sheriff's face and knew he was dead.

"What's out there?" he asked, standing up.

Yates moved to one window, and Clint went to the other one, on either side of the door. They saw the same thing. Across the street a bunch of men were behind cover, all with rifles trained on the jail.

"You thinking what I'm thinking?" Yates asked.

"Yeah," Clint said, "looks like we made the wrong decision."

FORTY-TWO

"Inside the jail!" a voice called.

Clint opened the door a crack and called back, "We can hear you."

"Send Sawyer out."

"That the Sawyer Gang out there?" Clint asked.

"That's who we are!"

"I'd advise you men to get on your horses and ride out of town," Clint said. "The federal authorities will be here any minute."

There was a moment of silence, and then the voice called back, "It'll only take a few minutes to shoot that place up, and you with it. Send Sawyer out!"

"Not a chance."

Clint waited for the man to say something else, but instead a hail of bullets struck the jail. He slammed the door closed, and he and Yates hit the floor with their hands over their heads. Glass shattered and lead chewed up the walls and the desk and everything on them. The prisoners were safe because they were in the back room, but they could certainly hear what was going on.

"What the—" Lacy said, sitting straight up on his cot.

Sawyer smiled and said, "My boys are here."

When the shooting stopped, Clint lifted his head and looked over at Yates.

"You all right, Gil?"

"Yeah," Yates said, "I'm not hit."

Clint looked up at the windows, which had no glass left, and saw that they had wooden shutters with slits in them for guns.

"We've got to get those shutters closed," Clint said, "and then fire back to keep them from rushing us."

"Okay."

"You take your window, and I'll take mine. Ready . . . go!"

They sprang up from the floor and each closed the wooden shutters. Immediately, the shooting started again, but the thick wooden shutters kept the bullets from coming into the room.

Both Clint and Yates drew their handguns and fired back until they were empty. When they stopped, so did the shooting across the street.

"That gives them something to think about," Clint said. "Reload."

While he reloaded he saw a gun rack on the wall with six rifles in it.

"We need those rifles."

Yates went to the rack, then turned and said, "It's locked."

"Damn," Clint said. "Check the desk for the key."

Clint looked outside while Yates did that.

"What are they doing?" Yates asked.

"They're waiting."

Clint heard drawers opening and closing, and then one slammed.

"No key."

"Watch them," Clint said. "It might be in the sheriff's pocket."

Yates went to his window, and Clint went through the dead man's pockets and came up with the key. He went to the rack, unlocked it, and took down a rifle. He checked it and found it loaded.

"Catch," he said, tossing the rifle across the room. Yates turned just in time to catch it.

Clint took another one down, checked to see if it was loaded—it was—and went back to his window.

"We're ready for them now," he said.

"What do we do if they rush us?"

"We shoot them."

"All of them?"

"Well, as many as we can."

"Right," Yates said.

"Hey, the jail! Adams?" the man across the street yelled.

Since there was no glass in the windows anymore there was no need to crack open the door.

"What do you want?"

"We want Sawyer!"

"No chance."

"You haven't had enough yet?"

"Bring some more and see," Clint called back.

"Is that smart?" Yates asked.

"What?"

"Goading them."

"I'm not goading them," Clint said. "I'm show-ing confidence."

"Oh," Yates said, then muttered, "sounded like goading to me."

Clint raised the rifle, sighted on the man who had the least cover, and shot him.

He looked at Yates and said, "That's goading."

Before Yates could respond, there was another volley of shots.

FORTY-THREE

"He shot Powell dead!" Styles shouted.

Too bad, Billy July thought, one less supporter for Sawyer.

"We'll have to rush them," he said.

"Some of us could get killed," Turner said.

"Or they could kill Sawyer," Styles chimed in.

That would really be too bad, July thought.

"How else are we going to get them out of there?" July asked.

"We could burn them out," Turner said.

"That would kill Sawyer," July said. "We've got to do something just in case Adams was telling the truth."

"About what?" Styles asked.

"About somebody coming from the prison."

"You think he is?" Turner asked.

"I think he could be," July said, "and I don't think we have time to wait and see."

"So we rush 'em?" Turner asked.

"We should," July said, looking around, "but I get the feeling some of us might not want to."

• • •

174

Yates looked at Clint and asked, "Can I try?"

"Sure," Clint said. "Pick the biggest target, or the clearest."

Yates nodded, sighted, and fired. Clint saw a man spin and fall. He wasn't the biggest or the clearest.

"Show-off," Clint said, but he was impressed.

"Damn it!" Styles yelled. "They got Charlie."

"Don't yell," July said. "If we're going to rush them, we better do it now."

He looked at Styles, who looked nervous.

"That's the Gunsmith in there," he said. "And who knows how many other men he's got?"

"He's got one," July said. "We killed the sheriff."

"What about deputies?" Styles asked.

"If there were any, they'd be here by now."

"So there's just the two of them?" Turner asked.

"That's my guess."

"I don't want to get killed because you had a bad guess," Styles said.

At that moment Kendall came over.

"What are we gonna do?"

"Kendall," July said, putting his arm around the big man's shoulders, "we have to rush that building and we need somebody to kick in the door."

"I can do that," Kendall said.

"I know you can," July said, "but I still need

some men who will rush with you and me. Think you can find any?"

Kendall looked around at the other men and said, "They'll go with us, Billy, or face me."

July smiled, patted the big man on the shoulder, and said, "I like having you around, Kendall."

Kendall looked surprised and said, "Thanks, Billy."

"Sure."

"They're getting ready to rush," Clint said.

"Can we stop them?"

Clint shrugged and said, "Maybe half."

"And then what?"

"Then the other half get us."

Yates looked at him.

"I don't like that."

"Me neither."

"So what do we do?"

Clint turned and looked back toward the cells.

"We improvise."

FORTY-FOUR

"Everybody ready?"

Kendall looked around.

"Everybody's ready, Billy."

"Okay," Billy July said, "let's go!"

Kendall headed for the jail first, followed by Styles and the other men. As Turner started across, Billy July grabbed his arm, holding him back until the others were on their way. Turner frowned at him, and then July released him and nodded.

Billy July was the last one to start across.

"Here they come!" Yates said and moved away from the window.

The door slammed open as Kendall put a big boot to it. He rushed into the jail, followed by several other men with their guns drawn. They stopped short when they saw Clint Adams standing behind Jeff Sawyer, holding his gun to Sawyer's head.

"What do we do?" Styles said out loud.

Yates was behind Clint, his gun also drawn.

All eleven of the remaining gang members couldn't fit in the office, so July pushed through them and entered.

"You're finished, Adams," July said. "Kill him." The order was directed to anybody.

"What the hell are you doing, Billy?" Sawyer asked. "Don't you see this gun at my head?"

"Can't let him get away with that, Jeff," July said. "You know that."

"You're here to free me," Sawyer said, "not get me killed."

"Kendall!" July said.

"Yeah?"

"Kill them."

Kendall looked confused, then appealed to Sawyer. "What do I do, Jeff?"

"Get out," Sawyer said. "Wait outside, all of you. They have to bring me out."

"That won't work," July said.

"Why not, Billy?" Sawyer asked.

"Adams said help was on the way."

"Adams is a liar," Sawyer said. "I'd tell you to go ahead and rush him now, but if you do that I get the first bullet."

Too bad, July thought.

"Kendall!" Sawyer snapped.

"Yeah, Jeff?"

"Get everybody out of here."

"Stay where you are, Kendall," July said.

Of all people in the room, Kendall looked to Clint for help.

"I don't know what to do."

There were four members of the gang in the room: July, Kendall, Styles, and Turner. The others were outside, and suddenly there was shouting and shooting.

"What the—" July said.

"Stand fast, Billy!" Clint shouted.

July looked around and saw that Clint was now pointing his gun at him and the other three. Yates had his gun on Sawyer.

"You, too, big man," Clint said to Kendall.

"What's going on out there?" Yates asked.

"We'll find out in a minute," Clint said, watching the four men.

Suddenly, the shooting stopped. Everybody in the room was just waiting to see what would happen next. Suddenly, a tall, well-built man wearing a sheriff's badge pushed his way in and stopped short.

"Clint Adams?" he asked, looking around.

"That's me," Clint said.

"What's going-on?"

"These men were about to give up their guns," Clint said.

The sheriff looked around, and Clint caught Billy July's eye.

"Weren't you?" he asked.

July hesitated only a moment and then said, "Put your guns down, boys."

• • •

Later, when the cells were filled with the remaining members of the Sawyer Gang, Clint sat in the sheriff's office with Yates and Sheriff Page Walker. The body of Sheriff Walters had been removed.

"My deputies and I were sent in from nearby Odell County when you contacted the authorities at Huntsville," Walker explained.

"I thought they didn't believe me."

"Apparently they didn't, because they sent me a telegram to come in and check it out. I guess it's a good thing they did."

"I guess so," Clint said. "Will you take charge of Sawyer and the other two prisoners?"

Walker nodded.

"We'll take them in, Mr. Adams," he said. "I'd advise you to ride ahead and square things with the authorities in Huntsville."

"We'll do that," Clint said.

He and Yates shook hands with the sheriff, and then left the office.

"You ready to ride to Huntsville?" Clint asked Yates.

"Ready as I'll ever be."

On the way to the livery to retrieve their horses, Clint said, "I want to thank you for your help, Gil."

"Thanks for the chance, Clint," Yates said. "I learned a lot, but I do have a question."

"Yes?"

"What would have happened if Sheriff Walker and his deputies hadn't arrived?"

"That's something we can only guess at, Gil," Clint said.

"I guess it would have been a mess," Yates said.

Clint nodded and said, "I guess you're right."

Watch for

THE TEN YEAR HUNT

160th in the exciting GUNSMITH series
from Jove

Coming in April!

If you enjoyed this book, subscribe now and get...

TWO FREE

A $7.00 VALUE—

If you would like to read more of the very best, most exciting, adventurous, action-packed Westerns being published today, you'll want to subscribe to True Value's Western Home Subscription Service.

Each month the editors of True Value will select the 6 very best Westerns from America's leading publishers for special readers like you. You'll be able to preview these new titles as soon as they are published, *FREE* for ten days with no obligation!

TWO FREE BOOKS

When you subscribe, we'll send you your first month's shipment of the newest and best 6 Westerns for you to preview. With your first shipment, two of these books will be yours as our introductory gift to you absolutely *FREE* (a $7.00 value), regardless of what you decide to do. If you like them, as much as we think you will, keep all six books but pay for just 4 at the low subscriber rate of just $2.75 each. If you decide to return them, keep 2 of the titles as our gift. No obligation.

Special Subscriber Savings

When you become a True Value subscriber you'll save money several ways. First, all regular monthly selections will be billed at the low subscriber price of just $2.75 each. That's at least a savings of $4.50 each month below the publishers price. Second, there is never any shipping, handling or other hidden charges—*Free home delivery*. What's more there is no minimum number of books you must buy, you may return any selection for full credit and you can cancel your subscription at any time. A TRUE VALUE!